MW00936566

Don't Judge A
B😈😀TY
By Its Cover

The Blessing and The Curse

by Pamela Chapron

CHAPRON PUBLISHING

LOS ANGELES, CALIFORNIA

Published and Distributed by:
Chapron Publishing
5482 Wilshire Blvd
Suite 376
Los Angeles, CA 90039
www.chapronpublishing.com

Cover Design: Steven Shelby
Formatting: starkbiz@sbcglobal.net
Second Printing, April 2010
10987654321

ISBN 978-1-514-78092-3

*I dedicate this book to every woman
who has ever been judged based upon
her beauty, breasts, booty or brains.*

ACKNOWLEDGEMENTS

First, I give thanks to Almighty God for allowing me to endure all of my trials and tribulations. The challenges I have faced in my life truly gave me the strength to become the person I am today. I also thank God for placing the right people in my path at the right time. Thank you David Mims for believing in my idea, even before I did! Thank you, Spirit From 4uentertainment, for supporting me. I give special thanks to Donna Dunn for being the angel that answered my prayer on New Year's Day. I thank author and inspirational life coach, Darnella Ford, for doing exactly what she is here to do—teach, inspire and motivate. She helped me to fall in love with something besides a man. I feel in love with myself and my project. Now, extra special thanks to my wonderful family who have always reminded me that I should have been rich a long time ago because of this "booty." To all of my family, I just want to say that I FINALLY sold this booty—not your way but my way! I love you guys with all of my heart!

Prologue

RIGHT LIGHTS BEAMED DOWN on Ida Mae as she lay flat on her back with legs wide open. She screamed, cursed, and even bit an attending nurse who was trying desperately to hold down her flailing arms. In excruciating pain, tears and sweat poured from her face. Positioned so the baby could come out easily, she lay upward in the bed but fought to stand up, pushing against the nurse's resistance to pull her back down.

Ida Mae had already given birth twice over so she was familiar with the pangs of childbirth, but found herself questioning why the pain was so much more unbearable than she had remembered. She knew the baby's head would be large, but this was ridiculous. The doctor began to pull the baby out of the womb with a puzzled look on his face. "What's this stopping us from pulling the baby out?" he asked.

"Get this fucking baby out of me, doc!" screamed Ida Mae. "What the hell is going on? How come it won't come out?"

"Something must be wrong," the doctor said. "Well…I'll be damn! It's her booty."

"What the fuck did you say?" Ida Mae's husband, Sonny, asked the doctor.

"Oh no! No! No!" protested the doctor, "I'm not talking about your wife. I was talking about your baby's booty! It's keeping the baby from coming out!"

"Have you ever seen anything like this before?" Sonny asked the doc. "A baby with a big booty like this? What do you think, doc?"

"We thought from the ultrasound that the baby's head was going to be large," said the doctor, "but it wasn't the head…it was the baby's booty."

"It looks like I might have to do a C-Section," said the doctor. "Nurse Betty, can you call Dr. Davis and tell him I need him immediately to help me perform an emergency C-Section?"

The room hushed to a still silence and replaced the joy of the occasion with grave concern. "We need to do this quickly!" snapped the doctor. "Ida Mae is about to pass out!" At first glance it was apparent that the baby's head was hanging out of the womb, but the booty wouldn't let go.

Dr. Davis finally arrived and looking at the situation, he whispered to the other doctor, "Damn…I have never seen anything like this in my life."

Sonny began to grow in anger and was consumed by worry for his wife and child. He did not understand what they meant when they said, "The booty is too big."

Ida Mae was in so much pain that in growing desperation Sonny wanted to slide across the room and punch both of the doctors in the face, but instead he opted for "I will be right back." Sonny knew he could not punch the doctor so he went to take a smoke in the waiting room to keep from going to jail. Excusing himself, he remembered from earlier in the day when they walked by the nurse's station he had overheard the ladies at the nurse's station talking about his baby's booty. Sonny's mind was wondering what the hell was happening. Sonny had babies before. He had also seen other babies come into the world, but he had never experienced anything like this before. He heard of a baby's head getting stuck, but never the booty. He just couldn't understand it.

Seeking comfort, Sonny called his mother to help calm his nerves. He was torn between excitement and concern, wondering if his wife and baby were going to be okay. After Sonny left the room, the doctor gave Ida Mae some stronger pain medication, and made a fine incision in her pelvic area to pull out the baby. Once the baby was actually out Ida sighed with relief, but was shocked to see the enormity of her baby's butt.

Ida Mae turned to the doc and said, "What am I going to do with this big booty baby?"

"I have delivered so many babies into this world, but I have never seen a baby with a booty like that," the doctor told Ida.

Ida Mae asked the doctor, "What I am going to do with this big butt baby?"

The doctor turned to Ida Mae and said, *"Don't Judge A Booty by Its Cover."*

chapter

1

 *M*y mother went through so much pain having me that every time she looked over at me all she thought about was how painful her labor had been. After that she started calling me her "big booty baby." It took her a whole month before she named me Mia. She said she wanted to name me Big Booty, but she knew my Dad would not like that. He wanted me named Laura after his Mom, because I was dark-skinned and my grandmother was black as night. Everyone used to say how much I looked like her. I did not like her because she was so black, and I thought that was ugly. In looking back, I realize I was just programmed by society not to like myself.

I remember when I was about twelve years old and I heard my mom talking on the phone to one of her sisters, and she asked about us kids. My mother told her how pretty my other sisters were but when speaking about me she said, "That little black one is all right."

I cried all night thinking that my mom really didn't like me because of my skin color, and that's why I hated when anyone said I looked like my grandmother. I really never looked at her so I never saw any of her features. I grew up always feeling ugly because my family called me, "Blackie." Deep down inside, I hated me. I hated the name my family called me. Still today, people judge you because of your skin color and even your own family members tear you down.

I really never believed I look like my grandmother till she passed away and my father gave me a copy of her obituary. That was the first time that I really looked at her. And that was also the first time I really saw me. In my family I was known as the black little girl with the big booty. I used to think something was wrong with me. As I got older, I started to develop another personality that didn't care anything about what people felt. That was Juicy, my booty and alter ego.

Juicy is not your normal alter ego. Juicy is a bi-polar personality that I have had to fight with most of my life. I didn't meet Juicy till I was 15 years old. She hibernated for years, and on a day when I least expected, out of nowhere she started talking. She damn near started speaking in tongues.

What?

Okay. Let's not get carried away so soon—more on that later.

Every woman has a Juicy. It is that other person who comes out of us ladies when we go out to Christmas and holiday parties and get drunk—and forget who and what we did the night before.

I remember one day this guy called and asked to speak to Mia. I said to him clarify which Mia he wanted to speak to, "last night's Mia or today's Mia?"

"Last night's Mia," he didn't hesitate to say.

"She's not in," I said abruptly and hung up the phone.

I wasn't being rude—just honest. I knew that last night's Mia was "Juicy" and not me. Juicy is so different than me. She doesn't give a damn about being judged. Juicy is everything people think a booty should be. When I go out to parties, Juicy wants to stay after the parties, but I take Juicy home and smother her.

Juicy hates Mia. In return, Mia also hates Juicy. They didn't start out this way. They began as "friends," but they ended as enemies. Somewhere along the way, they took a wrong turn. Juicy wants to own Mia, but Mia belongs to herself.

5

Juicy tells her story from the rear view of life. Mia tells the story from the front view of life. Juicy sees the world different from me.

I'm Mia—not Juicy.

In her defense Juicy reminds me, "You don't see what I see. You only can see a small part of the world looking at you. I see the whole world looking at me."

Juicy hypnotizes men.

They are drawn to her, and then Mia runs them away.

Juicy loves to fuck and to suck and get that money. She knows the power she possesses and loves to use every ounce of it. Juicy only comes alive when I drink Gin or Vodka. So why drink? It's a long story and I don't want to bore you with the details, but here's the deal: I got a thing for Gin and I got a thing for Vodka. They're my two best friends. They take the pain away. You know the pain, right? Everybody's got it. Some have more than others. I have my fair share. Now I don't want to get all weepy on you because you and I just met, but like I said—I got a thing. Don't judge me. Don't judge my booty. So let's get on with it, okay?

I just wanted to be loved and recognized for my brains, not my booty. But my booty always seemed to win out. By the end of this journey, you'll understand what I mean by that. I want to be humble but here's my truth—I'm beautiful and my body is to die for. Some days it has its perks and some days it doesn't. It doesn't mean a damn thing when my booty is all people see. They're staring at my outside walls—which means...they don't really see me.

Animal attraction. A one night stand.

A fuck fest free-for-all.

Call it what you want. They don't see me.

And even though I love to dress up every day like a model or a movie star, deep down inside I know it's just an illusion. Sometimes I get desperate and wish I could step out of this cover and just be average. But I can't because I'm scared. I don't know who I'd be without the attention. That lust. Those perks. I don't know that other

6

person. I've never met her before. I've never been a kin to ordinary.

But I can tell you this much I know is true. My heart is made out of pure gold. I love the world and the world loves me. But I'm locked away—somewhere inside, behind and beneath it all. I live in the shadow of Juicy. But it wasn't always this way. No, it wasn't always this way. Let me take you back to the beginning.

I would like to introduce you to my Mama.

chapter

2

IDA MAE WAS MY COLD-BLOODED mama. She was a beautiful young woman. She had a body to kill for with a tiny waist, voluptuous hips and big, thick legs from bottom to top. Her skin was caramel-colored with curly, black, silky hair. Everyone admired Ida Mae's body. Mature for her age, all her friends were much older than she was. Ida was very open-minded about sex. She was all about making that money. She believed that a woman had to do what she had to do in order to get what she wanted in this world.

Ida had a mouth like a sailor. She did not have to whip you—all she had to do was cuss you out. Her words were so piercing, every time the woman opened her mouth you felt like she had just pistol-whipped you. Ida's typical "Good morning" was a far cry from a Sesame Street episode. Let me give you a humble example.

"Get in here you little mothafuckers...and clean up this God Damned kitchen!"

"You little Bitches and Ho's!" she would scream at me and my sisters.

Ida was raised with the Word—the cuss Word that is. Her parents, and probably their parents, and all who came before and after, were some cussing son of a guns. Curse words were an acceptable standard of proper English in Ida Mae's house. You didn't know you were loved unless you were cussed out and then, in turn cussed somebody else out. It was the gift that kept on giving.

Chicago brought out the best and worst of Ida's gift. City living was no joke. Ida was as harsh and bitter as a Chicago winter. Chicagoans had life a little harder than people born in sunshine weather. Folks in cold weather climates seemed a little grumpy in the winter. They don't smile and damn sure don't seem happy.

In the brutal cold, people used to walk around with thick winter coats with their head and face all wrapped up. All you could see was their little bitty eyes peeking out of their head mask and they looked so mean. Then by springtime, when the sun started getting warmer, all you could see was people smiling and talking. Everybody was wearing less clothes and feeling good with their car windows down— guys hollering at the girls. It was a totally different attitude. There's something about cold weather that changes your whole damn attitude.

The weather makes folks tougher, harder. They could not go out and enjoy themselves all the time like Californians. Folks in the Midwest and on the East coast have to prepare for the winter. They hibernate like bears. They have to prepare to make money and plan something before the winter hits. Most Chicagoans know how to survive. When that windy city gets cold, people start to focus on what they need to do—no matter whether it's being that doctor, that drug dealer or that ho. Something about the cold weather breeds strength in people. Shit, they got to survive. So every man who dated Ida paid her.

Ida was baptized in making a man pay for it.

She took first, second and third communion on this shit every week.

You hadn't done shit—till you had a man take care of you.

You hadn't lived and you better not die—till you were steady on some Negro's paycheck.

Ida always said to her girlfriends, especially the ones with banging

9

bodies, "Girl, if I had your body, I would have EVERYTHING I wanted in this world."

"But Ida," her friends would declare, "you DO have a body, girl!"

"And that's why Bitch, I'm going to always have money," declared Ida.

"But I want to be in love with a man. I don't want to just take his money," her friends would say.

"Stupid God damned fool," cursed Ida. "What the fuck does love have to do with it? If you have to suck a dead dog's dick to get that money you should do just that."

Ida seemed cold, but she wasn't as cold as she seemed. She did love in her own way—she just saw life in a whole different way.

Now my daddy, he comes from another whole cloth all together.

chapter

3

MY DADDY'S NAME IS SONNY. He was born in Louisiana but raised in Watts, California. People born and raised in California are different. They seem a little happier—more laid back. The beautiful sunshine in Los Angeles makes you believe life is like a bowl of cherries—a Fantasy Island or a La La Land where stars are born and made. Everything from the trees to the people had some kind of plastic surgery. Everybody wants to be beautiful at all times and at all cost. You are constantly in a competition match, and there's lots of peer pressure. The attitude of people is, "Why work? The day is beautiful. Let's just go to the beach and pretend."

Sonny was a handsome man, a half-breed type. He always looked like a major player, and was a big time drug dealer from Los Angeles. He always had money. He was so cool that everyone thought he was a pimp. He had long curly hair that the ladies pressed out for him, so it looked like he wore a perm. He stood about six feet tall with broad shoulders. He wore pinstripe suits, the Super Fly kind and had the ladies flocking to be with him.

My father tried to be slick, but he really was the trick. With all of his might, he tried his best to be a pimp but it just wasn't in him. His heart was too kind. So instead of him getting everything from the ladies, he would end up giving his last dollar to any woman he put his dick into.

My father believed in giving women his money, and he loved to take care of his main women. He always felt a woman should get paid for her time. He always said if he had a pussy he would be rich. I guess you could say that both of my parents had a very open mind.

Sonny already had a wife with two kids before he met my mother. He left his first wife in Los Angeles and went back to Chicago, where he already had another lady.

Ida Mae was just 17 years old when she met my dad. He was friends with Ida's older sister, Mary, and her husband, Bill. She was my beautiful auntie, who was something like an angel. Mary stood about 5'9" with hair down her back. It was beautiful red hair. She was always a sharp dresser catching from head to toe. She was both stylish and domestic. Mary and her husband loved my mom like she was their child. She basically raised my mom because my grandmother had 13 kids. My aunt Mary was one of the oldest and my mom was the youngest of all the kids.

My aunt Mary threw this big, old wild party and that's where Ida Mae and Sonny made their first introduction. At the time, Sonny was ten years older than Ida Mae.

"Ida," said Mary the morning of the party, "Bill invited this sharp Cali guy to the party tonight."

"For real?" questioned Ida, one brow raised in excitement. "Hold on Miss Fast Ass…" cautioned Mary, "I know you like those California people but stay away from him, girl…you hear me?"

Ida offered a mischievous grin.

"You hear me talking to you, girl?" pressed Mary. "You're too young for all of that. Stay away from him. You hear?"

Okay Bitch, Ida thought to herself, but responded, "Sure sis. Whatever you say."

That evening she adorned herself in a tight fitting black dress, which showed off her Coca Cola curves. Her breasts were pushed up in the dress and spilled out so far that her titties greeted you long before the rest of her did.

Later that night, the party was on and popping. The music was jamming and Ida started to move her body in a seductive way.

That was the early stage of laying the trap. She was going to use her booty, thighs, breasts and whatever body part that was not already committed to another project for this one. She was going to hook Sonny from California, and then she was going to sink him.

Ida had been drinking most of the night and was starting to get a little tipsy. Now, Mary didn't mind Ida taking a swig of alcohol every now and again, as long as she didn't get too carried away. Mary just wanted Ida to be careful. She always wanted to give Ida the freedom to be herself. But at this point, Ida had gone way past being herself and had become somebody else—a drunken fool, perhaps. Or maybe not. Don't let the smooth taste fool you—Ida was *always* aware. And she was aware that she had to keep her eyes on the prize. And this time around, California was the prize. She always had big dreams of living in California because most people back then thought Cali was the shit. Some still do. So Ida Mae saw this as the perfect opportunity for her to get to Cali and go with someone who had lots of money.

She saw her "prize" leaning against the wall talking to her Uncle Bill. She also saw that she had competition. Her "prize" was surrounded by a flock of desperate women—as desperate as Ida herself—to hop on the next thing smoking to Cali. So Ida slinked her way across the room, drink in hand, to meet the man.

"Introduce me," she whispered to Uncle Bill.

"You can't handle him," Bill said to Ida Mae, "he's out of your league, little girl."

Ida Mae laughed it off cause she knew that he was the one who needed to watch out for her and not vice versa. Within moments, Ida had a strong arm around her, pulling her away from the scene and into the kitchen.

"Come on and help me with these drinks," suggested Mary. "Baby, please don't do anything you would be sorry for later on," cautioned Mary.

"Oh, I ain't gonna be sorry," promised Ida. Mary gave Ida a stern look of disapproval.

"Sis…I'm damn near grown. I can do what the fuck I want to do," boasted Ida, leaving the kitchen in a huff. By the time fast ass Ida made her way back to Sonny's corner, he was already surrounded by a whole lot of estrogen. Women from all over Chicago were putting the moves on Sonny. It looked like every bitch in town was trying to re-locate to California, and Ida knew she had to be on top of her game to catch this sucker. With no time to waste, she grabbed Uncle Bill and pulled him to the side.

"Tell me everything you know about Sonny," she insisted. "What?" asked Bill, slurring his words.

Shit, Ida thought to herself. His drunk ass is no good to me now.

"He's loaded," assured Bill.

Ida perked up when she heard the word loaded.

"How loaded?" she inquired.

"Rich as shit," said Bill, tipping over to the side. "His family owns a whole bunch of the gas stations in Cali," said Bill.

"Gas stations!" blurted Ida, as the whites of her eyes turned green with black dollar signs. "Damn! I hit the jackpot! You mean his family owns crude oil???"

"Guess so," slurred Bill.

"Like the Black Beverly Hillbillies, huh?" Ida questioned. And with that, she didn't wait for drunk Bill to respond. She pushed past him and barged right up in the middle of Sonny's conversation.

"Dance?" she asked.

That was a bold move for Ida because she didn't know how to dance worth a damn.

"I don't really know what I'm doing," she said, implying that her rhythm might be whack.

"Oh, I think you know exactly what you're doing," he insisted. "I don't really know how to slow dance," she said.

Sonny slid his arms around her waist and sucked her in like a slow vacuum. It was so rhythmic and melodic that Ida almost lost her balance. For a moment she forgot who was zooming who. Shit. Sonny was good but Ida was better.

Before Ida could fall into Sonny's arms or his pocketbook, the music picked up and Sonny started gyrating his hips, dipping and flipping—and damned near tripped Ida in her four inch heels.

"Shit!" she screamed out, trying to catch her own ass lest she fall face first right onto the dance floor.

"How old are you, girl?" asked Sonny.

"Old enough to know better," she said with a sly grin, "and young enough to do it all."

Ten minutes later Ida Mae accidentally lost her virginity.

Uh oh.

❧

One week later Sonny left for Los Angeles without Ida Mae. Ida was devastated.

Her man *and* her money had up and left town. But Ida Mae wasn't about to give up that easy. No way in hell. It was time to play a Wild Card—the only one left in the deck. And with that she put a 911 call into Sonny from California with GREAT news: *Guess who's having a baby?*

It was as easy as that—and Ida Mae was on her way to Los Angeles.

chapter

4

OW—BETWEEN YOU, ME AND all of the African Wildebeest, Ida was no more pregnant than the Pope, but a girl's gotta do what a girl's gotta do. Ida did feel bad, but a little guilt wasn't enough to keep her in cold ass Chicago. Ida reasoned that every woman got a "husband" by lying about being pregnant. Coming up pregnant was a guaranteed "marriage certificate" and so far, it looked like things were going along just as Ida had planned.

But on the other hand, Ida's sister, Mary, was not so supportive of Ida's decision to move on.

"I don't know…," she just kept repeating, standing over Ida spilling a room full of tears as she packed up all of her belongings.

"What are you so upset about, Mary?" Ida asked her in between sobs.

"I just don't trust him, Ida," said Mary, "you might just be rushing into a whole lot of nothing!"

"We getting married," boasted Ida. And with that Ida begin to spin around a giant circle in the middle of the bedroom and sing.

The only thing I know—Sonny's a millionaire.
Kin folk said, "Ida move away from here."
Said California is the place you ought to be.
So I loaded up my shit and I moved to Beverly—Hills that is…
Hair weaves.
And movie stars.

Ida grabbed one large suitcase, and did one final spin in the little bitty room she had been sleeping in and shouted at the top of her lungs, "Good bye! Now let's go!" And with that Ida was out the door, leaving Mary standing in the background shaking her head.

It was a short trip to the Greyhound bus station. All the way there, Ida had both eyes out of the window saying goodbye to the old tore down trees, raggedy ass should-have-been-condemned buildings, the old drunkards standing by the corner liquor store with one foot on the sidewalk and the other foot in the grave. All the while, Ida Mae's head was bouncing up and down as Mary tried to duck and dodge potholes the size of the deep end of the Grand Canyon.

"Damn Mary," scolded Ida, "I'm going to miss all this beautiful scenery."

Mary rolled her eyes and cared not to respond.

"See you later, suckers!" she screamed out the window.

"Ida Mae," scolded Mary, "get your big head back in this car."

Mary rolled up to the front of the Greyhound bus station and turned the car off. But there was no sense in doing that because the minute the wheels rolled to a stop, Ida's ass was out on the sidewalk and already at the ticket counter.

"Ida!" screamed Mary, "ain't you going to kiss me goodbye?" Ida turned around and blew Mary a kiss the size of all of California. "See you in ten, maybe twenty years!"

❧

The bus ride to Cali was long and brutal, but Ida stayed in good spirits thinking about fine ass Sonny and his exaggerated bank account.

On the day Ida arrived into Los Angeles it was a perfect day—sunny and warm. No humidity. The skies were a beautiful blue and the palm trees were swaying in a gentle breeze. Ida paid particular attention to the architecture of the city—the buildings were brand new. The streets almost seemed to ride like black velvet and it seemed that they were stretched out to eternity. They were wide and inviting and almost seemed to whisper, "Come…come… drive down me."

Ida sat back in that raggedy seat and mumbled to herself, "Aaaahhh…this is the good life. All my life I've dreamt about this place."

When the bus rolled to a stop, Ida Mae knocked down old people and children to be the first one off the bus. She couldn't wait. And the second she touched ground, she caught a glimpse of Sonny, who was waiting patiently at the bus stop for her. But when Ida spotted him, she had to do a double take.

"What the hell?" she said to herself. "What is he wearing?"

A closer look revealed a different side of Sonny. He was wearing an extra, extra bright yellow shirt with a big Hawaiian flower on it. And he had the nerve to be wearing some matching pants. They had a big green palm tree reaching out of the back. "What the fuck is he wearing?"

What happened to sharp dressing Chicago Sonny? He had blown away in the wind or maybe he was hiding beneath those wide-legged yellow pants.

Ida felt a little disappointed in how he looked, but her mood was quickly recaptured when she thought about the money. Ida was sophisticated-looking, wearing a tight fitting skirt and a silk blouse. She and Sonny seemed like the "odd couple" if this was his everyday kind of look (and it probably was). But then again, Ida did a quick reality check and realized that Sonny could have been wearing a turtle shell and as long as he had some dough—she knew everything was going to be all right.

Sonny greeted Ida with great enthusiasm. He even gave her belly a "gentle rub" and asked, "How are we today?"

We my ass, Ida wanted to say. She felt like exchanging it for, "How's my money doing?"

Sonny grabbed her suitcase and led the way towards the car. Ida started licking her lips. She had never ridden in a convertible before. She wondered if it was a Rolls Royce or another one of those fancy

Italian sports cars. Imagine the look on her face when she saw a "pimped out" 1960's Cadillac.

"What the fuck?" she mumbled to herself again.

The car was a loud metallic blue with long, shiny fenders and gold painted—not plated—I said painted rims. When Ida sat down her silk blouse was catching and running on all the velvet. On the passenger's side, some kind of way, a nail was sticking out and it damn near gave Ida a mastectomy when she sat down. Her delicate blouse up and ripped, on the spot.

"What the fuck?" she said out loud this time.

"Oh....Oh baby...." said Sonny apologetically, "watch out for that nail!"

"This is some bullshit," she mumbled beneath her breath, still not wanting to upset him, because after all—she knew she was about to 'get paid' and didn't want to act out and end up back in Chicago, which was Ida's worst nightmare.

"Can you take a run by the beach?" she asked.

"Sure," he said with a big 'ole smile, thinking about Ida's big old legs and thighs. *I can't wait to hit that again*, he's thinking to himself smiling, *you can have whatever you like.*

Within thirty minutes of Ida's arrival to Los Angeles, she was standing on the edge of the Santa Monica Pier. "Oh," she said to herself, "life is good again."

"How you like California, baby?" asked Sonny, trying to get fresh with Ida in public.

"I love it, Sonny!"

"Are you ready to be my wife and give me my beautiful baby?" he asked.

Ida paused a beat, cause she was no more pregnant the Pope, remember?

"Yes," she said stuttering a bit, hoping like hell that she could actually get pregnant quick, fast and in a hurry. It was nine months and counting, and she was already short on some weeks. Shit, the way Ida's math was coming up—she was hoping every egg she had was dropping down this week.

"Let's go have sex!" she suggested.

"Hell yeah!" he said, eyes as big as saucers. *I knew I had a hot one,* he thought to himself, *but got damn. She's a horny little bitch.*

"Let's go on to the house, baby," said Sonny.

"Okay," agreed Ida. But it didn't take too long before Ida remembered her inheritance—the gas stations? Remember, his family owned a whole empire of oil wells. Ida didn't even know Sonny's last name but as far as she was concerned—it was Abdul or some shit like that. She imagined both of his parents wearing long veils, Jesus sandals and reading Muslim literature as their private chauffeurs drove them all over town.

"Baby," said Ida real sweet-like. "Before we go to the house and I rock your world....how 'bout we roll by your family's gas stations?"

"Oh yeah baby..." said Sonny with an enthusiastic spark in his voice, "you want to see the gas station?"

The ride to the 'gas stations' seemed longer than the whole bus trip from Chicago to Los Angeles. It seemed like Sonny was driving extra slow so Ida could enjoy the scenery.

Fuck the scenery, she wanted to say. *I'm trying to check on my money.*

Within minutes, they were rolling down a street that didn't seem as inviting as the streets she was accustomed to traveling. This street seemed short, narrow, cramped and raggedy. She wondered whether or not she had left California by accident, but again, no need to rock the boat, so she just sat back real polite.

Sonny was just smiling and grinning. He was all teeth when he pulled into this little, itty, bitty, raggedy, tore down, limp-dick, looking gas station. The station was so small it had one pump with a pile of dirt around it.

The sign on the front door said "Open" but it was deserted as hell. Sonny's father was working the cash register from the inside. When we pulled up to the front, he looked more like he was making a desperate plea for one or two customers to come by that day. His father looked old and white, broke down and tore up.

Where's the oil Sheik? I wanted to ask. *Where are the Jesus sandals and the fancy cars? Who's the old white man behind the counter?*

"What the fuck?" she asked out loud.

"What's wrong honey?" asked Sonny.

Ida started to shrivel in size, going deep inside of herself. Her California dream was evaporating under the weight of a new reality. How was this one pump going to support Ida's new lifestyle? This one raggedy ass pump would have to let go of a whole lot of oil to keep Ida in the life she had already dreamt about living.

"That's daddy," said Sonny, pointing to the old shriveled up man in the window.

Ida did a slow wave and her favorite sentence mumbled beneath her breath. "What the fuck?"

Within moments Ida's blood began to boil, probably just like that cheap crude under this one raggedy ass pump. But she was still wearing that smile trying to pretend to be happy. She was trying to figure out what to do.

Should she run back to the bus station?

Put her tail between her legs and go home?

Admit defeat and call the whole thing off?

Or does she hold on till they get to the next gas station? "Can I see the others?" she asked.

"Other what?" asked Sonny, looking stupider by the minute. "Other gas stations BABY," said Ida with a bite.

"This is it…" he said, "ain't no other stations."

"What the fuck?" screamed Ida. "What the fuck? You said your father owns gas *STATIONS* in California."

"You must have misunderstood," he said, "when I said *STATIONS*… I meant one.

"My brother-in-law told me you owned a lot of gas stations!" "Oh Ida," said Sonny, "Bill was drunk talking all that mess. He was showing me how to bait those desperate Chicago women…"

"So what you saying, Sonny?" asked Ida. "I was the catch of the day? It was all lies?"

"Not all of it," he said. "We have a gas station in the family."

"This is a long ass way from an oil empire!" she spat.

"So, was it all about the money, Ida?" he asked.

I wouldn't have parted my legs like the Red Sea if I knew you were a broke Niggah, she said to herself, but it came out sounding more like, "No baby…it wasn't about the money." Ida Mae crossed her arms as rings of smoke seeped out of her nostrils. She was fuming mad. Ida began to choke on her own breath as she gasped for air, trying to hold on to what was left— obviously now—*nothing*.

"I got something to tell you," said Ida.

"What?" Sonny asked.

"I lost the baby right before I got on the bus."

The jig is up, she thought. *Fuck it.* Ida thought if she couldn't have a dream—neither could his broke ass.

"What Ida?" he asked, seemingly devastated, but not half as devastated as Ida was. "You didn't tell me."

"I didn't want to disappoint you, Sonny," she said trying to sound meek.

"Well damn," said Sonny. "What are you going to do now?"

No oil empire. No inheritance. No baby.

Forget about the maidservants. No Beverly Hills.

Bye Bye Sammy Davis. Damn.

Back to life. Back to reality.

Back to being broke ass Ida.

chapter
5

FTER THE FAIRY TALE ENDED, Sonny and Ida traded in Beverly Hills for a nice bedroom in his so-called house in Watts, California. It was a little one-bedroom guest house that was nothing like the Beverly Hills mansion Ida dreamt about, but hell, she did have some privacy—with the only drawback being that it was an unfriendly place to live because Sonny's mother was NOT feeling Ida at all.

"She's a God Damn lie," Sonny's mother told him when she met Ida. "That girl ain't pregnant."

Shortly after Ida moved in with Sonny they married and eventually Ida did get pregnant because after all—they kept fucking, so it was bound to happen. The loving couple had three little girls, and this is where I came in. *Remember me?* I was the one with the head hanging out of the womb, but with a booty that wouldn't let go.

Sonny was courting the Columbians and Ida was being serenaded by Rodeo Drive. Ida could shop till she dropped, and Sonny didn't mind spending thousands a week to keep her happy.

On one particular afternoon, Sonny called Ida unexpectedly.
Uh oh.

The jig is up, Ida thought. Maybe Sonny's tired of me spending up all of his money. Maybe he realized that I spend way more on my-self than I do on those damn kids.

The jig just might be up.

Sonny picked up Ida in his car and they made their way through the ghetto and kept on going—all the way to the Westside…

"Baby, why are we driving so far West?"

Within minutes, Sonny was turning down one of those pretty, wide streets that begged—*come drive on me.*

"Baby, we're driving into another whole league," said Ida, noticing all of the beautiful palm trees, freshly cut lawns and lovely rose gardens. Ida also noticed that the residents were wearing three piece suits and not bulletproof vests like they did back in Watts.

Oh damn, she thought. Ida's mind was racing. *What the fuck is he driving through all these white neighborhoods for?*

"You okay, baby?" asked Sonny, "you looking mighty nervous." "I'm good," she said out loud but to herself she's thinking, *I'm more scared than a mother fucker.* Sonny slowed down the car and parked right in front of this beautiful home. He jumped out of the car and said, "Baby…this is your new home." Ida was blown away. She couldn't believe it.

Sidney Poitier–

Guess Who's Coming to Dinner on YOUR street?

One week later the whole family moved into this spacious new home. This house was one of the biggest on the block. It had fancy chandeliers, a dream-like swing set, Jacuzzi and a swimming pool. And you know Ida bought the best furniture money could buy.

Life was good again.

Then the next day, it rolled over on its side. 5 a.m.

Monday morning.

The cops stormed our house and arrested my father for selling drugs.

It was the end of an era.

The end of a dream for Ida Mae.

They shackled my father in handcuffs and that was the last time I saw him, at least for a while.

❧

We stayed in our home till all of Sonny's money dried up or Ida Mae spent it up.

Ida would get dressed up every week and go visit daddy in jail. We would always ask, "Momma, where you going?"

"I'm going to visit your daddy," she said with a big 'ole smile.

"Where's daddy?" we'd always ask just to hear her usual lie, I mean reply. "Your daddy's off to sea."

She must have thought we had the word moron taped on our foreheads.

She always tried to pass off tragedy as something other than what it was. Everything had a double meaning and she never wanted to face reality, but eventually, reality faced her and we wound up selling everything we owned and moving back to Chicago.

chapter
6

*I*DA WAS IN A BAD MOOD that day. She was threatening to "beat our ass" for everything past breathing. The bus ride was long and miserable. Everybody on the bus could see the giant red letters on Ida Mae's face that screamed—

Broke Bitch Here!

I finally saw a little "humility" in Ida. She looked broken. "Momma…when are we going to get there?" I asked. "We been riding this bus for almost four days and I wanna see Auntie Mary."

"You little ungrateful big booty bitch…" snapped Ida, "we'll be there soon enough."

Goodbye pity, I said to myself.

Déjà vu.

Been here before.

The buildings looked even more run down than they did before and the trees were leaning a little closer to the sidewalk. The condemned buildings STILL hadn't been torn down. The streets were filled with cranky people and raggedy cars.

It was the same place.

Different people, but they were all doing the *same* thing.

When the old beat down bus pulled into the bus station, there was Mary, waiting in the lot with a big 'ole smile. Ida just sat back, took a deep breath and rolled her eyes.

"Oh Lord God help me…" she mumbled beneath her breath. "Momma," I screamed "is that Auntie Mary?" I asked, pointing at the lady with the red hair. Although we had never met our Auntie, it felt like we knew her because she and Momma talked every single day with Momma bragging about some shit to Auntie Mary. She really loved Mary and had several pictures of her sprinkled throughout the house.

"That's her…" said Ida, lips all curled up and drawn to the side.

"You don't seem *happy* to see Mary?" questioned my oldest sister.

"I'm happy heifer….shit," said Ida.

"Smile Momma," I said, tugging at her arm, "we back in your hometown."

After the bus parked, I think Ida Mae was the last person to touch down on the ground. We all ran off the bus and straight into Aunt Mary's arms.

"Oh my God!" screamed Mary, "look how beautiful you girls are!"

We smiled like we knew it was true.

"Where's your Momma at?" asked Mary, looking around for Ida. In fact, we all started looking, waiting for Ida to get off the bus. "I don't know," said Ducky, "she was right behind us."

"Ida Mae?" yelled Mary. "Ida Mae?"

Two minutes later, Ida slowly came around the back of the bus. She was walking real slow and looking real pitiful, head hanging down, hair uncombed, raggedy.

"Ida Mae?" questioned Mary, eyes wide open with disbelief. "What's wrong with you, baby? You home with family…don't worry about nothing. I got you and these kids."

On the outside Mary offered empathy, but on the inside she was saying to herself, I knew that mother fucker was *nothing but nothing in the first place.*

✨

Mary's house was a beautiful two-bedroom home on the south side of Chicago. It was so neat you were scared to sit on the couch, which she kept covered in plastic. She was so clean you could see yourself on the floors.

Mary gave my mother back her old bedroom. It was a little bitty, 300-square-foot hole *(a far cry from the 3,000 square feet she just left back in Los Angeles)*. Ida was grateful because it beat sleeping on the streets, but she was very depressed and spent most of her days sleeping.

She went from shopping to sleeping, and Mary stepped in and took more responsibility in raising us. Mary was heavily involved in our daily affairs while Momma slept…and slept…and slept.

Mary prepared our breakfast in the morning and our dinner in the evening. She commanded my sisters to clean up, scrub the hallways, bleach the toilets, but when it came to me—she catered to me. She made me feel very special.

It was during the time that we lived with Aunt Mary that all of us girls started developing. But we were all growing in different directions.

NeNe's breasts started enlarging. Ducky's breasts and feet got bigger.

My hips started expanding and my booty was getting bigger by the day. It wasn't a huge surprise because Ida saw it coming when my ass got stuck in the womb, remember?

Now here's the deal. When it seemed like everybody kind of "evened-out" my butt didn't get the message; it just kept growing and growing. Sometimes, I would take a bath and catch a peek of the rear view in the mirror and I wanted to say, *"Hold the hell on! Who are you and where are you going?"*

Life started getting kind of weird. It all started on the very first day of school. My sisters NeNe, Ducky and I were getting dressed. When I put my pants on I heard all of this laughing and cackling in the back-

28

ground. I turned around only to find Ducky and NeNe pointing at how big my booty had grown.

"Your booty looks like a balloon in those pants!" said NeNe. "Your tits look like two balloons in the front," I said right back. "I'd rather have the tits so at least I could see them coming," said Ducky.

"Well, you don't have anything going or coming…flat-chested!

"No booty! All I see is skin and bones!" I yelled.

"At least I ain't a big booty freak!" screamed Ducky.

Ouch.

That hurt.

That was enough for me. I ran out of the room, dragging my booty behind me, and ran into the kitchen where Aunt Mary was making our breakfast. Uncle Bill was already at the table, like always. If he wasn't drunk—he was eating. When he was eating—as soon as he got finished he was drinking. He altered between both worlds. Food and booze. Booze and food.

"Girl," said Uncle Bill, "get some milk out of the icebox." "Okay," I responded and headed that way but before I could get to the refrigerator, I caught the angry eyes of my Aunt Mary shooting piercing looks between Uncle Bill and myself. I didn't know what to make of it.

"Bill," Mary said sharply under her breath, pulling his attention away where it had been placed firmly on the backside of my rear end. But he was busted.

Ooooh….Aunt Mary caught you looking at my booty, I wanted to say but didn't. *You ought to be shamed Uncle Bill.*

"Sit down Mia," directed Aunt Mary, "I'll get the milk *myself*," she said.

I did as she asked me to do and quickly took a seat. Uncle Bill's head was buried in his cereal bowl and he was pretending to eat dry cereal to take off the heat of getting busted.

"When you get out of school today," said Mary, "We're taking a little trip to the mall—you and I."

"Just me by myself?" I inquired, "What about Ducky and NeNe?"

"Oh no," said Mary taking a sip of strong black coffee, "this is something especially for you." I was so excited about going shopping with Aunt Mary that it was hard to keep my attention on school. When Ducky and NeNe learned about my 'big day'—they were pissed they couldn't go.

"Why you get to go shopping?" asked NeNe with attitude.

"Cause I'm cuter than you," I said in gest, "me and my big 'ole booty."

"That ain't fair…you get to go shopping and we don't," said Ducky.

Deep down inside I knew the girls were right. What could Aunt Mary want to buy me that she wouldn't buy for them? Everything was split down the middle when it came to us getting stuff. Nobody got anything without everybody getting something. My curiosity was getting the best of me.

After the school bell rang, I ran outside of the building and there was Aunt Mary—parked right out front! Ducky and NeNe were slow to follow with their lips all twisted up because they were mad that I was going shopping. I hopped in the front and they hopped in the back.

"Mary," I asked so excited, "what are you going to buy me?"

"You'll see soon enough," she promised.

"That ain't fair!" said Ducky, "Are we going to the mall with you?"

"No, I'm going to drop you girls off first," said Mary, "and Mia and I are going to the mall."

"That's some bullshit," NeNe whispered under her breath. "Don't feel bad, girls," said Aunt Mary, "you'll each have your day."

"Why can't our day be today?" pushed Ducky.

Aunt Mary shot them both one of her sharp looks and everybody knew that meant leave it alone. It was probably funny to watch us rolling down the street—me in the front grinning right along with Mary and Ducky and NeNe in the back with their lips poked out and arms crossed against their chest.

Mary dropped them off and they both jumped out of the car and slammed the door. They didn't even bother to say goodbye, but I made sure I rolled down the window and yelled, "See you later suckers!"

"Mia," cautioned Mary, "it's not nice to tease or brag…your momma can tell you more about that."

By the time we made it to the mall I was about to bust with excitement. I couldn't wait to get my present. As we strolled through the mall, Auntie Mary noticed all these grown men staring at me. I always noticed people looked at me different but I didn't know why. Aunt Mary couldn't stand it—it was pissing her off the way all these older guys were looking at me. Some of them even seemed like they were trying to flirt. I looked a lot older than my real age, which was nine years old. They probably thought I was about 14 with my booty and all.

Before I could get a good look around, Mary snatched my arm and pulled me into Sear's Department Store. We walked towards the juniors department and I could see myself in all these cute dresses, but we passed that shit right up and kept walking.

"Aunt Mary," I said trying to tap on her shoulder, "we just passed up all the cute dresses…"

"Never you mind about that," she said and just kept on walking.

Oh.

Okay, I thought to myself. Maybe it's cute pants instead.

But we were heading straight for the lingerie department.

Oh shit, I said to myself. *We came here to shop for her.* Ain't nothing over here for me.

She went straight for some big bloomers and pulled them up, holding them high towards the sky. "Come here Mia," she said.

"Let me see if you can fit these."

Who me?

"Come on…come on," insisted Mary.

Slowly, I walked towards her and she handed me these big, old, thick panties with a lot of elastic in them. They were so hard. They didn't want to bend at all.

"What is this?" I asked dumbfounded, "this is too big for me."

I didn't come here for no panties, I thought to myself.

"These are not panties, baby…" said Auntie Mary, "this is a girdle."

A girdle?

Girdle??

What was I gonna do with this?

"I never heard of a girdle, Aunt Mary? What is it for?" I asked. "A girdle is something that holds your booty in when you walk so it won't jiggle so much," said Aunt Mary.

"What, my booty jiggles?" I asked. She nodded.

"Does NeNe and Ducky's booty jiggle too?" She shook her head.

"Can we buy one for NeNe and Ducky too?" I asked. She shook her head and smiled.

I wanted to burst into tears and Auntie Mary could see I was struggling with the whole plastic, hard panty. I knew I was different, but my Auntie wants me to cover up with a girdle? I must be more deformed than I even thought.

"I'm trying to protect you," said my Aunt, "you'll understand when you get older."

"Is there something wrong with my booty?" I asked her. "Child," she said, "let me tell you a story about a woman named Saartjie "Sarah" Baartman."

Aunt Mary went on to tell me the story of Sarah, otherwise known as Hottentot Venus, who lived a long time ago. She was a beautiful African woman from the Khoi tribe in Africa. In fact, she was the most beautiful of her tribe, so beautiful that the Europeans promised the king of her tribe that if they would let them take her, they would make her very wealthy and she would be able to come back and help her tribe. So the king sold her to the Europeans believing that they were being truthful. Sarah was forced to entertain people by gyrating her buttocks nude and showing to the Europeans what was thought of as highly unusual bodily features. They put her in a circus freak show and they judged her because of her booty. Eventually, Sara caught a disease and died, but even after she died they stuffed her body and kept it at the museum for display for many more years until Nelson Mandela was released from prison, and requested her bones to be returned to Africa for proper burial.

This was a whole century ago. I was still so confused and did not understand so I asked, "What do you mean they judged her booty?"

"Baby," my aunt said, "most people are only going to look at your body and not care what's in your heart or mind. They would lust after you or even try to hurt you because of the way your body is built. I don't want you going through this so it will be better if you hid it now."

I dropped my head because it made me so sad. Why would people judge me because of my booty? It was in this moment that I could feel myself withering—going from a happy child to a shy one.

That day Aunt Mary bought the girdle, but I didn't want to wear it. And to make matters worse, she wanted me to put it on right there in the store. My bottom lip started quivering and within seconds, I broke out in uncontrollable sobs.

I wanted to protest, but I knew it would do no good so I surrendered and put it on. Aunt Mary smiled with approval.

As we walked through the mall it seemed that Aunt Mary was satisfied that she had hidden a part of me. She seemed at great peace that for now at least—all was well with her—but not with me. This was my first introduction to the world of insecurity and wondering how long I would have to hide it.

How big would it grow?

What else should I hide?

And who else will want to lock me away?

It was a vicious circle—I wondered where would it end?

On my way home, I was dreading the face to face with NeNe and Ducky. I knew they would be eager to see what Auntie had bought for me. And I was sure prepared to rub it in their noses— but it wasn't going to go down like that. Instead, it was about to be rubbed in my nose. I barely had the strength to lift myself up out of the front seat, and to make matters worse, NeNe was in the window watching and waiting.

Damn.

Damn.

I'm walking up to the front door looking like an old lady wearing a body cast, I mean booty cast. It was heavy and bulky and awkward to find my next step.

"Where's your present?" screamed Ducky. "And why you walking so funny?" asked NeNe.

"Leave her alone and get in there and do your homework!" chastised Mary.

"We want to know what she got!" said Ducky. "She got a panty garment…" said Mary.

"What do you mean a panty garment!" yelled Ducky. "A girdle, little girl," said Mary.

"A girdle!" shouted NeNe, "that big old panty bloomer grandma used to wear!"

Ducky busted up laughing and started pointing at my booty. "You wearing grandma's girdle!" screamed NeNe.

It was earth shattering—the shouts and screams as my sisters demolished me from the inside out, and I sunk smaller and smaller. But I tried to let them know they didn't get to me, so I tried to keep a happy face and pay them no attention.

"Now your booty looks smaller, Mia!" said Ducky.

"You don't look deformed in the back anymore," added NeNe.

"Girls," said Auntie Mary, "everybody is on homework."

With all of the commotion in the living room, Ida Mae woke from the sleeping dead and made a guest appearance in the living room.

"What's going on here?" asked Ida.

Momma? Is that you? I thought to myself. Momma had been sleeping so much we forget that we all lived in the same house. She had been so depressed over my daddy being locked up in the jail, I mean gone to sea—that she had barely contributed any motherly nurturing to us in the past several weeks.

Ida would wake up. Go to sleep.

Wake back up. Eat.

Poop. Say "good morning" or "good night" depending on whether the sun was shining or not.

Even Mary was surprised to see her.

"Ida?" Mary called, "how you feeling?"

"Mama…" said Ducky, laughing. "Mia's wearing grandma's girdle!"

"What?" asked Ida, confused by the statement.

"Look at her booty, Mama…it's smashed in," said NeNe, trying to force me to turn around.

"Leave my booty alone," I said pushing NeNe back. "Let me see…" said Ida.

I slowly turned around and Ida Mae's face turned beet red. She turned to Mary and said, "What the fuck you put my daughter in a girdle for?"

"Because her booty's jiggling…" defended Mary, "and older men are lusting after her."

"What older man?" shouted Ida, "You mean your husband Bill is looking at my daughter's ass?"

Insulted and hurt Mary responded, "I'm not even going to acknowledge what you just said to me, but if you don't care about grown men wanting to fuck your daughter then neither will I."

Ducky, NeNe and I were glued to their conversation wondering if they were getting ready to go to blows over it.

"What's the big deal about the girdle?" asked NeNe.

"Go to the bedroom!" screamed Ida, "I need to talk to your Aunt Mary in private."

We were slow to shuffle out of the room because we were curious.

"Your booty sure does cause a lot of trouble," said Ducky on the way into the bedroom. "Your booty got us on lockdown."

"Shut up, Ducky!" I said. "My booty ain't done nothing to nobody." When we went into the room, we pressed our ears against the wall and could hear bits and pieces of their "adult conversation."

"You trying to give Mia a problem with her booty," said Ida, "and there's nothing wrong with my baby's booty. She's blessed."

Mary didn't say anything.

"This is a special child," said Ida. "I knew she was different when she came out of me. Her booty is something to be proud of—not hidden behind a girdle."

"That's crazy talk, Ida…" said Mary, "that girl needs to be careful."

"Careful of what?" asked Ida, "she should show it to the world with pride. It might make her a lot of money…she might hook a millionaire with all that booty."

"So," said Mary, "You want to pimp your daughter?"

"I don't want her to be no broke ass, begging bitch," said Ida. "I want all of my daughters to be proud of what they got and to use what they got to get what they want."

Mary was beside herself. She couldn't believe what she was hearing.

"Listen Ida Mae," said Mary, "Mia's going to wear this girdle in my house. If you won't protect her—I will."

And with that, Mary stormed out of the room.

Uh huh… Ida thought to herself. *The bitch ain't trying to protect my daughter—she just don't want her husband dreaming about my daughter while he's fucking her.*

"You hear that?" asked Ducky, pressed against the wall. "Mama said we got to work with what we got to get what we want."

"What you working with?" asked NeNe, checking out her own body. "I got some big titties."

"What you working with?" Mia asked Ducky. "I'm working with my legs," said Ducky.

"Them skinny, bony legs…" said Mia, "don't look like you ain't got nothing to work with."

"Well give us some of that damn booty of yours," said NeNe. "It looks like you got too much to work with."

"Do you guys believe Mommy's gonna make us use what we got?" asked Mia.

"Yeah," said NeNe, "to get what we want."

chapter

7

ONE DAY I WOKE UP and realized we had been living with Aunt Mary for almost a whole year. Wow! It had gone by so quick with all of the new changes in our lives. Ducky, NeNe and I were adjusting to a new school, new friends and new family, but it seemed like Ida Mae was stuck in yesterday. All she did was sleep and wait for my dad to call. It seemed like Ida was sleeping somewhere around sixteen hours a day, give or take a few minutes for bathroom visits and showers.

It was really getting on Mary's nerves. She was sick of seeing my mom so sad.

"Ida," suggested Mary, "why don't you call your girlfriend and tell her you're back home now..."

"I've been home a year," said Ida almost choking on the words.

"Well," said Mary, "it's about time you got the hell out of the house. Don't you think it's time to start socializing?"

"My husband is doing time..." said Ida, "I guess it doesn't make any sense for me to do time too."

"Exactly!" agreed Mary.

"I think I'll call my old friend, Shirley, with her ho ass," said Ida. Ida really didn't want to be bothered with anybody else. She knew she would have a lot of explaining to do as to why she was back with Mary again.

Fuck it, said Ida. *I got to do what I got to do,* and with that she grabbed the phone and called Shirley.

"Hello," said Shirley.

"What's up homey?" asked Ida, "It's been a long time. How you been?"

"Is this who I think it is?" asked Shirley, "my rich ass girlfriend who moved to Los Angeles, got married, had kids and forgot about all her friends."

"Shut up bitch!" shouted Ida. "I could never forget about your ho ass…"

"I would love to see you…what are you doing tonight?" asked Shirley.

"Nothing," Ida said.

"Come on and go with me to this party…I got somebody I want you to meet."

"Girl, I haven't been out partying in so long…" said Ida. "Don't trip…" said Shirley, "It'll be fun. Get dressed. I'll be there in an hour."

❧

Later that night Shirley and Ida were at the club, catching up on old times and new times. Shirley was tripping off Ida's life in California. "Girl…" said Shirley, "I thought you guys were living the *good life* with all those gas stations I heard your man had…" "Girl…the niggah's family had one damn station. One damn pump, and one old ass father that ran everything."

"Get out!" said Shirley.

"But I had already fallen in love with him…" "Why is the niggah in jail?" asked Shirley. "He was selling that shit…" said Ida.

"What the hell, partner…you okay?" asked Shirley.

"I'm all right," said Ida. "Tell me about your friend. Who did you want me to meet?"

"A cool ass dude! You won't believe this one, partner," said Shirley, "this guy really does own gas stations out here and is super paid!"

Upon hearing the words, Ida's depression seemed to be lifted straight off her shoulders.

Could this really happen twice?
And better yet—
This time could it be for real?

That night Ida Mae and Shirley went to the bar. Shirley's man brought his "friend," but Ida was unimpressed because at first glance he was short and stubby.

"Is this the man you was telling me about?" Ida leaned over and asked Shirley.

"That's him," said Shirley, "Fine…ain't he?" Ida Mae turned up her nose.

"Partner," said Shirley, "look at those beautiful, light brown eyes."

Ida took another quick glance and noticed that his eyes were beautiful, but that was about it cause his stomach was no joke. It looked like he was about to give birth to twins, and Ida wasn't feeling that because she was used to Sonny's six-pack.

"Bitch," said Shirley, "don't be choosey now…he's staring right at you."

Ida quickly put her head down and asked Shirley, "does this mother fucker really own some gas stations, Bitch? Don't sell me no bullshit like Bill sold me."

"Ask anyone in here," blurted Shirley, "he's the man in Chi-Town."

Before Ida could gather herself, the short man with the big belly was right up in her face.

"Hi," he said showing all of his teeth, "I'm Clyde."

"Hi," said Ida forcing a smile, looking for any and all signs of wealth.

"Nothing like a fresh face in town…aren't you a beautiful lady?" said Clyde to her, but thinking to himself, *and some big, new tits in town, too.*

"Why…thank you," she said, sopping it up like biscuit gravy. "Can I buy you a drink?" he asked.

"I believe you can," she said. "Cognac please."

After Ida got two good drinks in her, she was starting to feel him. After the third drink, he was getting skinnier by the minute. Especially once he opened his wallet and she caught sight of a wad of cash and every major credit card. *He sure is fine*, she whispered to herself, *but what about Sonny?* Ida started to feel guilty for even entertaining someone other than her husband.

"I can't do this," Ida said leaning into Shirley, "I'm married." "Bitch, how are you going to take care of your kids?" she asked Shirley. "You sitting there thinking about your husband but he can't help you from a jail cell."

"I know…I know…" mumbled Ida. "I gotta get a job."

"Doing what?" asked Shirley. "You never worked a day in your life. You might as well do what you know best…"

"Fuck it…" said Ida, "a bitch gotta do what a bitch gotta do."

Ida Mae was on top.

Clyde was on the bottom.

They were in Aunt Mary's basement and Clyde was a "moaner" so it seemed like Ida spent the whole night trying to keep Clyde quiet.

"Sssshhh…" she said, "you're going to wake up my family." But Clyde didn't care.

He just kept moaning.

And groaning.

This is some good shit, said Clyde as he exploded inside of her. Ida jumped off and quickly cleaned herself up.

He shook his dick off and got up and put on his pants. Ida didn't want to be too obvious, but she was sure enough waiting around like where's my money, fool?

"Can I see you again?" he asked. "Depends…" she said.

"On what?" he asked.

"My money is fucked up," she said. "How fucked up?" he asked. "About two hundred dollars worth," she confessed. "I got kids to take care of…"

And a date with Neiman Marcus tomorrow.

"You ain't got no man?" he asked. "He's locked down," said Ida.

And with that Clyde opened his wallet and dropped two hundred dollars on the table.

"See you next week," he said.

When he left Ida picked up the money and smelled it.

Sure did smell good.

She went from smelling dollar bills to nine months later smelling dirty diapers and baby formula.

Uh oh.

Ida Mae had a newborn and a trick was the daddy.

Uh oh.

For Real.

In the meantime, Ida was talking to Sonny every day on the phone. She talked her whole way through the pregnancy and not a word was said about her swelling belly.

"How you making ends meet?" Sonny was always asking. "Oh," she said, "I'm on that welfare system."

And some dick, too, but she dare not say that.

"Baby I know you miss shopping," said Sonny, "but when I get out you're gonna be able to shop again."

"Okay Sonny," she said.

"And I know you miss this dick," he suggested. "Uuummm hmmmm," she said with a half-smile.

Now, their next conversation went a bit different because there was a screaming newborn howling in the background.

"What's that noise, Ida Mae?" asked Sonny, inquiring about the odd sounds.

"That's the TV," she said. "It's a new show..."

"Damn," said Sonny, "sound like a real baby right there in your arms."

Real enough, she thought to herself. After all, Ida was breastfeeding her newborn son with the little belly and big pretty brown eyes.

"Stop tripping, Sonny," she said to take his mind off the conversation. But the conversation came back around again— about two days later Sonny and Ida were on the phone and about five minutes into their conversation, the baby started screaming.

"You must be watching that show again," said Sonny. "What show?" she asked.

"That show with the crying baby," he said. "Oh yeah," said Ida. "Hell of a show."

But it didn't last too long—the show. Ida had to come clean because every time Sonny called it seemed like it was feeding time, and she knew she couldn't keep telling him that it was a television show. She was terrified, not knowing how to tell her husband, but she knew she had to tell him something. Their next conversation was a full blown confession.

"When you coming to see me in California?" asked Sonny. "I don't know," said Ida, "it's complicated."

"What do you mean?" asked Sonny.

"I got something to tell you," she said trembling. "You can tell me anything," he said.

"Can I tell you I had a baby by another man?" she asked. There was stone, cold silence on the other end of the line. "Can I tell you that, Sonny?" she asked again.

Can I tell you that I needed help?
Can I tell you that I needed money for these kids?
Can I tell you how cramped we are in this little two-bedroom house?
Can I tell you that I did what I had to do—to make it, Sonny?

"Can I tell you that, Sonny?" she asked one more time. "I had a little boy and his name is Bobby."

"Are you in love with him?" he asked.

"What do you think, Sonny?" asked Ida. "I did what I had to do."

"Why didn't you get rid of it?" he asked.

"A lot of women die from botched abortions," she said, "and you know I never believed in doctors." Still silence. "And no, I'm not in love with him," she said, "he's married too." "Okay," said Sonny quietly, "I gotta go Ida…I got some big decisions to make."

"It was just about the money, baby," said Ida pleading, "you're the only man I've ever loved."

"You sure got a funny way of showing it," was all he said before disconnecting and leaving Ida hanging on her own end.

chapter

8

*I*DA AND SONNY DIDN'T SPEAK for about a year but things sure did change during that time. Ida and Clyde got real chummy and by the end of that year, we had two brothers, Bobby and Levi. They were born exactly one year apart. We couldn't understand how Momma had two babies with daddy off to sea, especially since she had never gone to sea to "see" him.

In the meantime, Ida kept calling the prison to talk to Sonny's counselor to make sure he was okay, but never got a return call. Sonny had disappeared into thin air. So Ida Mae had no choice but to continue on with her life and do what a woman had to do. In time, my sisters and I wondered what happened to daddy. Momma was not talking to him anymore at all on the phone and we had a lot of questions for her.

"Momma," I asked, "we miss daddy…why doesn't he call anymore?"

Ida's lip stiffened. She didn't know what to do with questions so at first she tried to shoo them away, but of course me, Ducky and NeNe wasn't going out like that.

"Is daddy mad at us?" NeNe asked. "Doesn't he love us anymore?" added Ducky. Yes.

Yes.

And yes, she said, trying to shoo us away again. But again, we weren't having it. "Did you tell daddy about our new brothers, Bobby and Levi?" I asked.

NeNe laughed because she was older and knew where babies came from and how they came. NeNe always tried to tell me and Ducky that Momma had laid down with another man and made both babies. NeNe swore up and down she saw them together one night. She said momma was making the funny noise that she always made with daddy and the short man with the big gut was squealing like a pig. But me and Ducky didn't believe NeNe, and that's why we wanted to talk to Momma so she could tell us what was really going on.

"What happened?" asked NeNe, "two new babies...no daddy?"

"No more phone calls," added Ducky.

"You little fast ass bitches," shouted Ida, "leave me the fuck alone. Daddy will be calling soon." And just as those words left her mouth it came true. The phone rang and Ida quickly answered. And guess who was on the phone?

"Ida Mae," said the familiar voice that made Ida's heart skip two beats.

Ida Mae was scared to death. She was missing Sonny something terrible and was so happy to get the call, but was terrified to tell him about the second baby. The first baby about did him in; she couldn't tell him there was another one. In fact, she tried like hell to hide it, and when she gave birth to Levi, she gave the hospital a fake name *(her sister's name)* so that the baby could be legally recorded as being my aunt's baby and not Ida Mae's. But of course, that too blew up in her face and Ida had to come clean for a second time.

Damn.

"How you been Ida Mae?" asked Sonny.

"I been real good," said Ida, sounding kind of shaky, especially when the newborn son, Levi, started crying in the background. There was a long, long pause in the conversation.

"Damn," said Sonny, "that baby sounds like it's still brand new. How old is that baby now?"

"Oh, that one is a year old," said Ida.

"What do you mean that one?"

"Sonny...can I tell you something?" she started out.

Oh damn.

Here we go again.

"Oh shit," said Sonny taking a deep breath, "you can tell me anything, Ida."

"Sonny," she said sounding pitiful, "can I tell you I had another baby?"

Did I tell you that I needed help?

Did I tell you that I needed money for these kids?

Did I tell you how cramped we are in this little two bedroom house?

Did I tell you that I did what I had to do—to make it, Sonny?

"Oh shit Ida," said Sonny, his voice dropping off into great disappointment.

"Niggah…" said Ida, "I ain't heard from you in a whole year! A woman's got to do what a woman's got to do!"

There was another long pause, followed by stone cold silence. "Are you telling me you had another fucking baby, Ida?" "Yeah," she said, "that's what I'm telling you."

"What the fuck, fuck Ida?" he said. "I'm calling to tell my wife I love her and that I will accept the first baby…but mother fuck Ida… you telling me you got a second baby."

"Yeah," said Ida again, "that's pretty much what I'm telling you."

"Fuck," said Sonny.

After a long pause Sonny took a deep breath and asked, "do you love this mother fucker…the one that you had this baby with?"

"No Sonny," responded Ida, "You're the only man I have ever loved."

"Who's this one's daddy?" he asked.

"Oh," said Ida matter-of-factly, "it's the same man." "What the fuck????" asked Sonny.

"A woman's gotta do what a woman's gotta do."

"I'm tired of hearing that shit, Ida," said Sonny. "You could have protected yourself."

"I tried to," she pleaded, "but it just didn't work out like that." "Damn," he said defeated, "So this mother fucker's taking care of you and my kids?"

"He helps out a lot," said Ida, while thinking to herself, *especially helps me in my long term relationship with Sak's and Neiman Marcus.*

"Guess what? He owns some *real* gas stations out here in Chicago."

"I don't give a fuck," said Sonny. "I'll be out of here in six months and I'm divorcing you."

"What?" screamed Ida, "you going to let two babies come between us? What kind of bullshit marriage is this? We got three kids together!"

"Bitch…" he said, "next week I'll call and you might have three kids by him at the rate you're going."

"But I don't love him," said Ida, "he's nothing but a trick."

"Yeah bitch…" says Sonny, "and you was the treat."

❧

That was their last conversation for six months.

Six months and one day later Sonny showed up on Ida Mae's doorstep.

Ding!

Dong!

Ida answered the door with both babies in hand—with Levi sucking the tittie and Bobby on the hip. Ida's mouth dropped when she saw Sonny standing on her doorstep with a shy smile. And though he looked hurt when he saw both babies, he was still filled with great affection for Ida. "Hi," she said, stuck somewhere between being embarrassed to see him and being excited to see him.

"So these are your babies, huh?" asked Sonny, stuck somewhere between his hate and his love for Ida.

"Yeah Sonny…these are the boys," said Ida.

"Where are my kids?" he asked, "I'm here to see the girls." "They're in the bedroom," said Ida. "Sonny, why haven't you called me? I'm still your wife."

"Bitch…" said Sonny, "you wasn't thinking about being my wife when your legs were cocked up in the air!"

"Sonny, I wrote you many letters telling you I was sorry, but you never wrote me back."

"I tore up every letter that came in the mail," he said. "Where's my kids, ho?"

"They're in the room asleep, Sonny." "Wake them up!" demanded Sonny.

Mary was drawn to the door by all the commotion and took one look at Sonny and frowned, "So when did they let you out?"

"Nice to see you too, Mary," Sonny said sarcastically.

"You meet your new boys…" she said, taking a jab right into his chest.

"Ida…get your sister…" said Sonny, "I just got out of jail and I don't want to go back."

Sonny walked past Ida and Mary and entered the house calling his girls.

"Mia! Ducky! NeNe!" shouted Sonny.

And we awoke that day to the familiar voice of our father. It was like Christmas Day all over again. No tree, lights or a feast— just daddy, but that was enough. He was our gift.

"Daddy's home!" we all screamed.

We all ran right into daddy's arms. We were so happy to see him.

"Daddy…you meet our new brothers?" asked NeNe.

"Yeah baby," said Sonny, "I miss you guys…dang…I can't believe how big you guys got! You're all so tall and pretty."

"The babies are getting big too," I said.

Sonny's face turned red and he was ready to explode, but he tried to change the conversation. "Damn…look at your ass, Mia!"

NeNe and Ducky started laughing, and I could feel myself shrinking.

"What have you girls been up to?" he asked.

"Just hanging out with our new baby brothers," said Ducky. "Mama makes us babysit all the time."

"Girls!" screamed Ida from the other room, "shut the fuck up!" "I gotta go girls…" said Sonny, "but I'll be back."

Struggling to hold back the tears and his fist, Sonny stormed out of the kid's bedroom and straight through the living room out the front door. Quickly, Ida passed off both babies to Mary and ran out behind him trying to convince Sonny of her love.

"Sonny!" she screamed. "Sonny!"

He stopped and turned around to face Ida, his eyes filled with tears.

"Where are you staying?" pleaded Ida, "When you coming back?"

"I ain't never coming back to see you!" he said, "but I'll be back to see my kids real soon."

He turned to leave again and Ida Mae grabbed Sonny's arm. "I knew you was a bastard! You're always leaving me and my kids! I hate you! I hate you!"

Sonny was on the verge of explosion.

"It's all your fault!" screamed Ida, "if your dumb ass had never got caught … none of this would have ever happened! You're a dumb motherfucker, son of a bitch!"

And with that Sonny turned around and smacked the shit out of Ida Mae.

One slap.

Two slaps.

Three.

Ida screamed—holding her face in pain.

"Sonny," she said pleading, "I thought you understood." A woman's got to do what a woman's got to do.

❧

Eventually Sonny forgave Ida Mae and they reunited as husband and wife. Sonny accepted the two boys and raised them as his own, but Ida realized that she had given birth to two "lucky charms" because their daddy really did own real gas stations. So, with Sonny's consent, Ida hired a family lawyer and took the boy's real father to court. She thought she was going to clean up on court day in child support payments. She and Sonny got all gussied-up for the court performance. But the joke was on Ida, because the boy's father was a powerful, influential man in the community and when it came time for the judge to hear the case, there was a whole courtroom filled with strange men.

"Who are these strange men?" Ida asked her attorney as he sat beside her.

"I don't know," said the attorney.

But they would all soon find out. The judge called the first witness who almost blew Ida Mae out of her seat when he stood up in the court and said, "I slept with Ida Mae." And then another stood up, "I also slept with Ida Mae."

"Don't forget me too, judge," said another stranger way in the back of the room.

"What the fuck?" said Sonny, turning to Ida Mae, who was actually astounded by what was happening because she had never seen any of these men before today.

"I don't know what's happening," she whispered to the attorney, "I never slept with none of these Niggahs….I only slept with that bastard over there," said Ida, pointing to Clyde, the gas station owner. It was then that Clyde turned to Ida and winked.

"Unless you come up with some proof of your own," said the attorney, "I don't see child support payments in your future."

"You mother fucker," said Ida beneath her breath, as she sat back shaking her head. She glanced at Sonny and wondered what he thought about these wild accusations. Sonny looked at Ida and offered a disappointing look.

Did she fuck all of these Niggahs? he asked to himself.

"I love you," mouthed Ida to Sonny, who just sat back and closed his eyes.

God, I hope she ain't fucked all of these Niggahs.

"Case closed!" said the judge, hitting his hammer on the desk. Translation: *No Money for You.*

And with that, Ida and Sonny went on with their happy lives. It was a life void of shopping, exotic trips and fancy gadgets.

Bye Bye Neiman.

Bye Bye Marcus.

Give my regards to Sak's…

Hello JC Penny.

Good morning Wal-Mart.

chapter

9

Five Years Later.

$\mathcal{B}$Y THE TIME I was 14 years old, we were back in Los Angeles. Ida Mae never felt good in her skin in Chicago so we came back to the West. When we moved back to L.A., I started pulling away from the family a bit and coming into my own.

I was young Mia—stuck between childhood and adulthood.

Smack in the middle.

I wasn't as shy anymore. In fact, I began to develop my own personality. I burned the girdle and everywhere I went boys, men, and old men were talking about my booty. They were staring at it, pointing at it and talking to it. My booty became the center of attention.

Ida Mae loved the attention my booty was getting because she saw potential profits in the form of my assets.

"When you get older Mia…you got to use what you got," she said, "to get what you want."

I never really understood it or accepted her philosophy, but it was always with me.

Use what you got to get what you want.

It was like a prayer or a chant in our house. It didn't take too long before all of the attention seemed to get out of hand. In one sense, I liked it because it made me feel special or unique. I was different than every other ho in my house. But on the other side, it was problematic because it stopped me from having fun, the kind of fun that young girls liked to have. Grown men were constantly "lusting" over my body, which made the adults uptight because they always had to monitor the attention to make sure it wasn't stepping over the line. And it seemed easy for men to step over the line.

How much can a grown man stare at a young girl's body before it becomes inappropriate? This was such a big deal that I couldn't wear my favorite pair of shorts, or my favorite jeans, but all of my sisters and friends seemed to have no restriction on their wardrobe.

I couldn't wear this. I couldn't wear that.

And damn sure couldn't wear the other. Why?

Because my booty was bigger than a grown woman's at the age of fourteen and it stood out.

Way out.

But I was always conflicted in my own body because I always felt like this body belonged to someone else. I couldn't be what people expected me to be in this body. Perhaps Ida Mae should have occupied this body instead of me. Later, this would become an important part of my journey.

Two Years Later.

By the time I was 16, my body was outrageous. I was very curvy. It seemed that women with curves who wore tight clothing were immediately judged as being a whore or a sex object, but I begged to differ. I had decided to wear whatever I felt good wearing. I had a preference for fitted clothing. I reasoned that if fat girls and skinny girls could wear tight clothes without being called a "whore"—then why couldn't I? But of course friends would have preferred me to wear a Moo Moo. All of my girlfriends were really jealous and they didn't like going places with me because of the attention I got. They hated when I wore my tight jeans. What I could not understand is the fact that they came to the parties with their tight shirts and big tits busting out. So what was the difference? I had no problem with that, but it was something about my butt that had everyone going crazy.

During this time, one of my best friends was named Trillion. I met her at school when I was 15 years old. I'll never forget the day I met her and she said her name was Trillion.

"Why do they call you Trillion?" I asked.

"Because I'm worth more than a million," was her only comment.

I knew in that moment that we would become great friends, despite the fact that Trillion was a lush at the age of 15. She always tried to cover it up with double doses of Listerine, but the liquor on her breath said "hi" to you way before the mouthwash did.

She had gusto and flavor. She was about the only girlfriend I had who was not jealous of my booty. She was a pretty girl with a high yellow complexion, but she also had her fair share of hang ups. She came from a dark-skinned family—black mama—black daddy—black siblings with no logical explanation for her high yellow skin. She never fit in with her family and was often judged or misjudged by her fair-skinned appearance.

Trillion and I had something in common. I felt as judged or mis-judged as she did. We had different 'outsides' but felt the same on the inside. This connection made us very close. But we were very different in one way. Trillion didn't give a damn about being judged and I did. I was overly-sensitive to the way people looked at me. No one ever knew because I did a pretty good job of putting up a decent front.

It's very hard when you are judged trying to get people to accept you for who you really are on the inside. We can't help the covering God gave us. Shortly after I met Trillion, we became good friends. In getting to know her better I realized that pretty girls can also be very insecure too. In fact, it seemed that the more attractive the girl was— the harder it was to live up to people's expectations. They don't know their own self-worth, and through Trillion's eyes I was able to see much of myself. Perhaps, I, too, struggled with my own deep seated issues of self-worth. Of course, I was too young as a teenager to know that. We all see through our own lenses so differently. I've heard that the prettier you are the worse you are inside—and sometimes I believe that.

People are always telling pretty girls they're so beautiful, and they take it in and drink it all up. But here's the joke—pretty girls think it's going to be so easy and that the doors open quickly, which they do, but the faster they open the quicker they close. We have to learn early on that life owes you nothing and that what you want—you have to work for it.

"What do you want to be after you graduate school?" I asked Trillion one day after school when we were walking home.

"Taken care of…" she quickly replied.

"You sound a lot like my Momma," I said. "Do you know Ida Mae?"

I busted up laughing but Trillion just looked at me clueless. "Don't you have any dreams?" I asked Trillion.

"Yeah," said Trillion with a smile, "I dream of being taken care of."

"Damn," I said shaking my head.

"Well, what do you dream about Mary Poppins?" she asked me.

"I want to be a lawyer."

"Sounds like a lot of work to me," said Trillion shaking it off.

"Girl, have you looked behind you, lately?" "What?" I asked, somewhat confused.

"With all that booty you don't have to go to school to be a lawyer," said Trillion, "that booty can get you the jury, the judge and the lawyer."

"Girl, are you crazy? I want to go to school and get an education," I said.

"We'll see after my birthday party this weekend just how educated you want to be," said Trillion, "with all of those fine, uneducated boys at my party."

If there was one thing Trillion was serious about, it was her partying. She had planned this wild birthday bash while her mother was going to be out of town for the weekend. She did have a lot of friends so I knew the party was going to be wild without adult supervision. Trillion had this hoochi friend named Chance who was wild as hell. I hated being around this girl and was always embarrassed to be seen with her. The funny thing about Chance was that she was always bragging about being a "virgin" but her mouth was anything but a virgin. It was broken in so many times because every other day she was in the bathroom on her knees working that mouth piece.

When I found out Chance was coming to Trillion's party, I wanted to back out. But it wouldn't have been cool for me to miss my girl's party, and it would just feed the rumor in Trillion's mind that I was "jealous" of Chance.

At the end of the day, Trillion and Chance were both sneaky and a lot faster than I was. They had a lot of lot guy friends, and Trillion even had this one guy she really liked who seemed like he was part of a gang. I wasn't a big fan of this guy, but I never said anything because I figured she knew what she was doing. "Trillion," I asked her on the day of the party, "are you a virgin?"

"No," she said, "But my momma thinks I am and that's all that matters."

From the looks of our outside appearances, people would assume that Trillion was Snow White and me, Darth Vader. But they were wrong as hell. Trillion was probably a freak and I was still a virgin. My body gave them the wrong impression, and my tight-fitting outfits didn't help clear up the misunderstanding.

❧

That night at the party, all of Trillion's gang member friends came over. We welcomed the guests into the back yard where we had decorated everything with these cool looking psychedelic lights flashing on and off. The table was filled with balloons and punch bowls filled with Trillion's favorite recipe of vodka and Hi-C punch Kool-Aid. The music was bumping and the DJ was playing James Brown's new record, "The Big Pay Back Got to Get Back."

It was hot.

I was leaning up against the fence and everyone was partying in front of me, urging me to join the party, but I was somewhat shy.

"Mia, come here and stop being a wallflower!" shouted Trillion.

I smiled but stayed pressed against the wall. Trillion didn't want me to be reserved, so she offered me a glass of her favorite punch.

"Take a swig," she insisted.

"Girl," I said protesting, "you know I don't drink." "This ain't nothing but some Kool-Aid," she said. "I know your slick ass," I said accepting the drink. "Just try it…" she said with a big grin.

So I did.

I took a swig, and it wasn't bad, so I took another. "It's good," I said nodding.

"Drink the whole thing!" she said pressing on the cup trying to tip it into my mouth.

After a few more swigs, or maybe cups *(I can't remember now)*, and I started feeling less like a wall and more like a flower.

Freeeeeee…

I started moving around a little bit, grooving to the music. Me and Al Green was getting along real good.

"You wanna dance?" some guy asked. I accepted his invitation and we moved out into the middle of the dance floor. In no time, the guy I was dancing with started rubbing all over me. He was moving kind of quick, but it didn't bother me much because he was kind of cute. The drinks kept coming and soon, I began to feel dizzy and my head started pounding. It was a very painful headache that came on without warning. I tried to play it off and keep on dancing.

Shit, I said to myself, *my head felt like it was about to explode*.

But instead of an explosion, it was worst—I began to hear voices.

Hey Mia…

Mia… Mia…

What the hell?

Who's talking? I asked myself.

Back here.

Behind you, Mia.

I turned around but I didn't see anybody. I looked at the guy I was dancing with but his mouth wasn't moving.

Shake me, Mia.

Shake me.

Rub me up against the guy you're dancing with!

What the hell? I asked again.

Shake me, you dumb bitch!

In that moment, I dropped my drink and ran into the bathroom, trying to outrun the voices that I kept hearing in my head. By the time I reached the bathroom, it was quiet again. I couldn't help but wonder if I was going crazy. I ran water into the sink and dunked my whole head into the face bowl. It was then that the voices started up again.

Hey!

Hey Girl!

It's me!

Turn around and look at me.

My name is JUICY!

I'm your BOOTY and I got your back!

I need you to listen to me…I can make you rich, powerful and get you everything you think you want in life…but ONLY if you allow me to be me!

I'm your best friend, Mia!

I see the whole wide world looking at you, Mia!

You have the front view of life and I have the rear view! I will call guys over to you, Mia.

I will rub up against the ones that need to be rubbed.

I'll suck the ones that need to be sucked.

I'll fuck the ones that need to be fucked.

Because a booty's gotta do what a booty's gotta do.

I ran out of the bathroom freaking the hell out. In the middle of my hysteria, I couldn't help but notice Chance down on her knees at the end of the hallway working that mouthpiece on one of the neighbor kids.

I made a dash toward the door, but the guy that I was dancing with grabbed my arm and was trying to talk to me.

What the hell?

I was ready to go.

I didn't even say goodbye to Trillion, I just got the hell out and ran all the way home. By the time I got there, I had calmed down a bit. Initially, I was terrified by what I heard—a talking booty named Juicy? As I laid down on the bed, my body began feeling sexually aroused.

What the hell?

It started feeling good. Real good. I felt like Juicy was a "bigger" part of me. I felt like Juicy was the confidence that took over my insecurities. Juicy felt strong where I had felt weak. Juicy KNEW she was beautiful but as Mia, I was uncertain. I kind of liked her crazy butt, but at the same time, I couldn't believe what was happening. And it got deeper. Later that night Juicy taught me how to touch myself. She showed me what to do, and how to rub myself. I did what she asked and I had my first orgasm. It was an explosion like the Fourth of July. I was making so much noise I hoped my sisters didn't hear me. As the liquor wore off and Juicy started to fade she promised she would be back…and teach me *more.*

❧

I woke up the next morning tripping. I couldn't believe what a crazy dream I had last night. I was talking to a crazy booty and it was answering. Or maybe it was me talking and I was answering. Or maybe I was just straight up drunk from Trillion's punch.

Later that day, I talked to Trillion and asked if I was acting strange last night.

"Girl," she said in a huff, "all I can tell you is that you ran out of the party like somebody was chasing you."

"After drinking your PUNCH, it did feel like somebody was chasing me."

Trillion laughed. It was a big joke to her. Everything always was.

She didn't take life too serious.

"Girl, who was that guy you were rubbing your booty up against?" she asked.

"I wasn't rubbing my booty up against nobody," I defended. "You talking about that fine guy I was dancing with?"

But before Trillion could answer, my phone was beeping on the other line.

"Girl," I said getting ready to click over, "Got another call coming in…I'll talk to you later."

I quickly clicked over. "Hello?" I said.

"Hello," said this deep voice, "may I speak to Mia?" "This is Mia," I said, "who is this?"

"This is Robert from Watts," he said, "I'm the guy you were dancing with last night."

"Robert from Watts…how did you get my number?" "You gave it to me last night, remember?" he asked.

I didn't remember giving him my number, but then again, I couldn't remember NOT giving him my number. What I do remember is that he was a cutie pie, and he wasn't a gang member like all of Trillion's friends. We hit it off right away and he kept calling every day. I never had a boyfriend so it was kind of fun to talk to somebody day and night. I would fall asleep every night with the receiver in my ear talking to Robert.

Finally, one day he invited me over to his house. "I want you to come see me," he said.

Watts? I said thinking to myself. Boy, I can't let Mama know I'm going on that side of town. She would beat my ass for sure.

"Okay," I agreed, "I'll come tomorrow after school." "Cool," he said, "see you then."

The next day after school was as adventure all its own. What happened was no small matter indeed. I caught about three buses to get to Watts from the West Side of Los Angeles. It took so long to get to Watts, I felt like I was going all the way back to Chicago.

Robert's house wasn't hard to find. In fact, it stood out like a sore thumb. It was old and needed to be painted. The house was purple with green trimming, and it looked like the paint was peeling off the side.

Dang, I said to myself, *this house sure is raggedy.*

Truth be told, the whole neighborhood was raggedy. Folks were standing outside their home and playing cards in their yards. But everyone seemed cool. Robert invited me to the back of the house which was the entry to his bedroom where it looked like he did a lot of entertaining under these red lights wrapped all around the door. His bedroom had this big sign that said, "Welcome to the weed room."

He had a red velvet couch that sucked you down all the way down to the ground when you sat on it. It felt like you were just swallowed up. You couldn't even get up without someone pulling you up. The room also had a weird smell to it. There were many big pipes, all different shapes and colors. It seemed like smoke was coming out of the pipes all by themselves.

What the hell?

The Temptations were playing in the background. I saw gin and Old English 800 bottles sitting on the table. Of course, Robert was tearing up some weed, and he asked me if he could give me a charge, but I didn't know what a charge was until he showed me. He hit a joint, inhaled the smoke, took my mouth and blew it into my mouth and said, "Suck it in, baby."

Okay.

I sucked it in and blew it back out. "How you like that?" he asked.

"I don't know," I said frowning, "aren't we recycling the smoke?"

He busted up laughing. "You are a fool!" he said.

"Yes," I said, trying to be very cool.

"Was that your first time trying weed?" he asked me. "No," I said lying. Obviously, it was.

Within minutes of me smoking the stuff, I felt like I was going to die. I never had weed but I knew about it so I was trying to pretend to be cool. I hit it again and started getting dizzy. Robert asked me if

I wanted something to drink and I said, "Yes." He asked did I want Old English beer or some gin, and I opted for gin and juice, remembering my girl Trillion's favorite recipe.

This was the second time I had drunk anything. I liked how booze made me feel. It seemed like I didn't have any problems of being shy or square when I drank. I fit in better under the influence of something other than me. I hadn't drank since that night at my girlfriend Trillion's party, but I really liked him and didn't want him to think I was a square. He said he was a DJ and asked what type of music I wanted him to play. I told him whatever he liked. I started getting very dizzy and this bad ass headache started coming on me again. I felt just like I did when I was in the bathroom at my girl's party. Then, I started to hear that voice.

Oh damn.

Hey girl!

Girl!

It's Juicy....

Oh no, I thought. *Here we go again.* I didn't want Robert to hear the voices too, or think that I was crazy, so I tried my best to ignore them. But the more I ignored them the louder the voice got.

Move closer to him! commanded the voice.

I moved closer and Robert was all over me. He started kissing me, rubbing and touching. He eventually made his way to my booty and started rubbing all over it. It was then that a voice rang out in what felt like a sonic boom inside of my head.

Yes! Yes!

Let him rub on that booty!

Open your legs!

Open your legs, Bitch!

I obeyed and opened my legs.

Let him feel on that koochie.

Let him feel it.

Put it on him....

And again, I obeyed. I didn't know why but the voice seemed like it knew what it was talking about. It felt like the boss.

Robert pulled out some lotion and started to massage my back and my booty. I felt like I was leaving the room and somebody else was stepping in to take my place.

Take your clothes off!

Take off your panties, girl!

Again, I obeyed. By now, it seemed like the voice was no longer speaking to me but *through* me. And it was here that I became an all-out, buck wild freak.

"Fuck me! Fuck me!" Juicy demanded.

"Whoa..." said Robert, taken back a bit as I begin to take his clothes off.

I opened my legs and laid back on him and let him kiss me all over my body.

"Give me that big dick, Robert!" shouted Juicy.

Robert listened to Juicy even better than Mia did. And not even a minute went by before that boy spread my legs open and pushed his dick inside of me.

"Fuck me in the back!" demanded Juicy.

Again, Robert was obedient and flipped me over and started banging me from the back.

"Mia...you feel so good!" gurgled Robert. "Call me Juicy!"

"Okay Juicy...." he said eagerly. "You sure do feel good, Juicy."

It took all of one minute and Robert was done. Shortly, after he pulled out I started to come down off the high, and then I didn't feel so good anymore. When it was all over I just laid there and started to cry. I was so confused.

"Don't be ashamed Juicy," he said, trying to take me into his arms.

"Juicy?" I cried out, "Why did you call me Juicy?" "That's what you told me to call you," he said.

Shit, I thought to myself. It must have happened again.

Something is really wrong.

Who and what am I becoming?

chapter

10

$\mathcal{F}$OLLOWING MY "SEX SHOW" WITH Robert, I withdrew into my own little world. It was dark, cold and lonely there. It felt like a rape, but it wasn't because I gave my consent. Who was to blame? Robert? Me? Juicy?

Two days later Robert finally caught up with me on the phone. Out of embarrassment, I had been avoiding his calls. But it was weird because he had asked me to be his "girlfriend" before I left his house that day and I said, "yes."

On the flip side, and there was always a flip side, I was excited to have a real boyfriend.

"Where you been?" asked Robert, when I answered the phone.

"Hiding," I said. "Why?" he asked.

"Embarrassed," was all I could say. "About what?" he inquired.

"What we did…"

"Don't worry…" he said casually, "I've done that a lot of times."

Oh great, I thought to myself. "I've never done it, Robert."

"Shit," he said, "you could have fooled me…all them tricks you was doing."

"Robert!" I scolded.

"Forget about it," he said, "You're my girl now." "Okay," I said, trying to move on.

"Why don't you come back tomorrow?" he asked.

"Okay," I said, easily convinced. It would be nice to see him again, I thought.

❧

The next day the grits hit the fan. I had no idea that my bus ride was going to take me on the journey of my life. I was about to get a real awakening in Watts, California. Hold on to your drawers, we're getting ready to go for a hell of a ride.

The raggedy bus broke down on the way to Watts and I was stranded on a curb where I had to wait for another bus. I was two hours late getting to Robert's and when I arrived, he was standing on his doorstep with fire in his eyes. He was looking like the devil itself coming to welcome me in.

"Hi," I said, with half-a-smile.

"What took you so long!" he screamed. "The bus broke down."

"Were you flirting with any guys?" he asked, "you sure are wearing those pants pretty tight."

"No!" I protested, "and these are the same pants I had on the night we met at the party."

"Boy," he said, "I bet all of those guys on the bus were staring at your booty."

Within seconds he was in my face. He ripped my purse out of my hands and began to shuffle through my bag, accusing me of collecting phone numbers.

"What are you looking for?" I asked becoming afraid. He was acting like a mad man. I had never seen him like this before. He was a totally different person than the one I had met before today.

He went inside the house with my purse still in his hands. "Give me my purse!" I insisted following behind him.

Once inside, I glanced into the living room and saw his mom and sister sitting on the couch watching the soap, *All My Children*.

I was trying to act cool and not let his mom and sister know that I was scared as hell and just wanted to get my purse and get as far from this wild man as possible.

"Hi," I said waiving to his mom and sister. "Hey," they both said at the same time.

"Are you Robert's new friend?" asked the mom.

"Yes," I said, but really wanted to say, *his soon to be ex-friend.*

"Do you want to sit down and watch some TV?" his sister asked.

"Sure," I said, thinking it would be safer with them than with crazy Robert. I quickly took a seat, but couldn't help but notice Robert pacing back and forth between the kitchen and the living room.

What the hell is he doing I thought to myself. Back and forth he went. Up and down.

Back and forth.

His mother was also watching this bizarre behavior and I could see that she was getting more and more irritated.

Back and forth he continued to walk. Minutes later, he called out my name. "Mia!" he said, "come here!"

I froze.

I really didn't want to go because I didn't trust his crazy ass but away I went. I entered the room slowly and gently eased my way over to his bed and sat down. I was steaming mad because I wasn't feeling a warm welcome today, but I tried to suck it up and thought maybe he was just having a bad day. Eventually, he returned my purse, throwing it back to me. It felt considerably lighter and when I opened it, I saw that he had removed everything but the wallet and a tube of lip gloss.

"What's wrong with you?" I asked.

He didn't answer, just kept doing his thing—going back and forth between the bedroom and the kitchen.

"Robert," I said, "why won't you talk to me?"

Back and forth.

Kitchen.

Bedroom.

Finally, his mother came and stood in the doorway. She had a very serious look on her face, like she was about to deliver some real bad news. I was waiting for some kind of devastation but all she said was, "young lady...you should leave now."

"Is something wrong with Robert?" I asked wondering what was going on.

"You should leave," she insisted.

"What did I do?" I asked.

"Nothing young lady," she said, "You *must* leave now!"

"Why?" I asked.

"Because," she said sternly, "My son is in the kitchen boiling some hot water."

"Okay…" I responded, "what does that have to do with me?" "He is going to throw it on to you!!" she said.

I could not believe my ears.

What?

What?

"Go now!" shouted the mom. I took one glance into the kitchen and saw Robert taking a pot of boiling water off the stove. Even though it sounded crazy to me, I decided to take the mother's advice and not wait around to see if Robert was going to boil some tea or boil me. Instead, I ran my ass all the way to the bus stop without looking back. I thought that crazy guy was going to come and chase after me. The bus was coming just as I approached the bus stop! Thank God. I really couldn't believe what his mother said about that boiling water, but I said to myself, "she knows her son much better than me."

❧

By the time I got home I was devastated. I was so confused. Was he really trying to burn me or was his mother lying just to get me out of their house? But he was acting very crazy and accusing me of such ridiculous things.

It was all too much.

I couldn't make heads or tails of it. How could the man that I was digging so much want to hurt me? And why was he so jealous? Was this what my Aunt Mary warned me about as a young child? About men judging me because of my body? I had a lot of questions but very few answers, which would only grow in number over the next few weeks.

Robert and I had stopped talking. He tried to call me several times and apologize, but I wouldn't take his calls—at least for a period of time. Then one day I realized, I had to call.

The past couple of months I had been sick in the morning and was throwing up all over the place. I didn't know what was wrong. But Ida Mae had a clue.

"You little Bitch," she said, "I hope you're not pregnant and if you are it better be Michael Jackson's baby!"

I was hysterical at the thought. I did have sex and we didn't use any kind of birth control. It wasn't entirely out of the question that I could be. The next morning Ida took me to the doctor's office where they tested me for everything from the Bubonic plague to an early pregnancy. The results came in immediately.

Guess Who's Having a Baby?

"So we're on our way to Michael Jackson's house, right?" asked Ida, "cause I KNOW this baby ain't by no broke niggah."

I was hysterical.

16 years old and pregnant.

You would have thought that my mother would have been more upset about me having a baby at 16 versus me having a broke niggah's baby. Obviously, this was not a good time to tell her that the baby's daddy lived in Watts.

"So what you got to say for yourself, girl?" asked Ida Mae, fuming mad. "If it ain't Michael's…it damn sure better be Tito's…"

"No mom," I said, "the baby belongs to the man I love… Robert."

"Robert who?"

"Someone I met at Trillion's party," I said.

"All that little bitch knows is bums and broke ass gang members," said Ida, "please Mia…tell me you're not pregnant by one of her friends." Mia was silent and the silence spoke for itself.

"You're a damn fool if you have this bum's baby," my mother said to me. "You ain't never going to be able to shop at Neiman Marcus."

"But I love him…" I said not knowing any better.

"You'll never be able to give this baby all of the things I gave you girls in life," said Ida boldly.

What life? I thought to myself. *She was busy giving herself the good life.*

It didn't matter to me what my mother said, I was going to move forward with the pregnancy. I felt very lonely and lost inside, but I knew that if I had this baby, somebody would love me. And that's all I really wanted was someone to love me—not necessarily to be somebody's mother. Big difference. It's easy to want a child's unconditional love—but in looking back, how could you love another when you can't even love yourself?

It was time to deal with the devil itself. I had to get Robert on the line after avoiding hundreds of his calls.

"Robert," I said.

"Mia!" he shouted. "Where you been?"

"Why haven't you returned my calls?"

"Robert…I decided to move on from you…"

"What?" he shouted, cutting me off.

"Robert…your momma told me you was boiling water to throw on me," I said.

"I would never do that!" he shouted, "I'm in love with you, Mia."

"Really?" I asked.

"Baby…you're the love of my life," he said, "I just don't want nobody else to have you."

"For real, Robert?" I asked.

"Yeah baby…you the only one for me."

Wow! His words made me feel so good. I felt like he really loved me. I had felt so alone most of my life and Robert and the baby would make me feel whole.

"Robert," I said, "since you feel so strongly about me…I have good news for us."

"What?" he asked enthusiastically. "I'm going to have a baby."

"My baby?" he asked.

"Yes fool…you're the only man I slept with." "That's great, Mia…" he said.

"But baby…my mother is not happy with this at all," I said.

"I gotta get out of here."

⚜

I dropped out of school and moved with my beloved baby's daddy and his family. His mom wasn't too happy but they supported Robert because he was the "golden child." As time went on, I got bigger and bigger and me and Robert got closer and closer. I really did love this guy. He filled up all of the holes in my heart, at least I thought so in the moment.

A few months later, I had a beautiful baby girl that I named Janiah. She looked like a caramel-colored Barbie doll with dimples and big locks of silky black curls all over her head. She was the most precious baby that anyone could lay eyes on.

For the first time in my life, I felt complete and whole. But it wouldn't last forever.

The first year was bliss.

The second year we began a descent into misery.

I had jumped out of the skillet and into the fire. Around the time of Janiah's second birthday, Robert began to act a bit strange. He's always been kind of intense, but he just started getting more intense as time went on. He was smothering the life out of me. I couldn't take a shit without him standing at the door offering me a tidy wipe.

Good Lord!

Can a girl have some privacy?

Robert was growing more and more insecure with the passing of each day. Pregnancy had changed my body dramatically. In other words, my stomach went down and all the baby weight shifted to my rear end. That started to bother Robert more and more. He believed that every time his friends came over they were coming over not to see him—but to stare at my booty. This made him crazy. He was always accusing me of wanting someone else.

Eventually, he started to beat me all the time. I really couldn't understand why he was so jealous of me. I really did everything in my power not to make him jealous, but it didn't work. If we were driving down the street and someone would happen to look at me in the car, he would slap me. I used to cry all the time. I actually wanted to die so many times. I just didn't know what I could have done for Robert to act like that. I knew I was nothing like he thought. I tried my best to hide the abuse from my family. But one night, it got too bad to hide.

One night Robert came home early from work and found me on the phone. I was talking to my brother. He heard a male voice and he snatched the phone right out of my hand.

"Who are you, homey...talking to my girl?" He didn't even wait for an answer. He just hung up the phone and started choking me and just before I went unconscious, he let go of my throat.

I started crying and ran out of the house into the street. He came after me and started calling me back.

"Mia! Mia!" he shouted, "I'm sorry."

I don't remember much else, just a long string of apologies.

I'm sorry.

I love you.

I'm sorry.

I'm sorry.

I love you.

And I always took him back.

It always worked. At least for a while but you can't change an abuser—you can only change yourself. But I didn't know that at the time. I only blamed myself for all that was happening.

It was getting more and more out of hand. I blamed myself. I believed I was the problem because of my looks but I always wondered if it was my booty. One time one of his friends was looking at my booty and he turned around and slapped me. I was so tired of the abuse and the apologies.

"I need some fresh air," I said to him.

"Are you going to call the police on me?" he asked.

"No," I said, "I love you. I just need to get some fresh air."

I left home discouraged and depressed. As I walked down the street, I passed the neighborhood liquor store and stopped. I thought about going inside and buying some gin. I hadn't drank in so long because Robert couldn't stand me and alcohol in the same room. He always said that when I drank I "turned into someone else." But I wanted to take my mind off all the troubles. The booze would do it. It would set me free, at least temporarily, from my troubles.

I opened the bottle, took a swallow and slowly began to guzzle the forbidden juice of pleasure. I started to think about all the ass-whoopings that I did not deserve and all the things he had done to me.

The more I drank the stranger I began to feel. There was a sudden, sharp pain in my head, and the subtle voice that spoke to me from the rear view of life.

Hey girl!

Hey!

Don't take that shit!

Go back home and kick his mother fucking ass!

I told you I got your back!

You're a weak Bitch, Mia!

You need me, Mia!

The voice was right and I knew it. I surrendered Mia to Juicy, as Juicy came front and center. She straightened both of us out, shook off the rest of Mia's self-pity and got on back home and burst in the room with a gangster attitude. "You hungry, baby?"

"Yeah," he said, "cook me something to eat, damnit!"

"Okay baby," Juicy said real sweet-like, "you can have whatever you like."

"That's more like it," said Robert nodding his head.

He came into the dining room and sat down at the table with a big grin on his face. He thought he was getting ready to get a meal fit for a king. He was licking his lips and nodding his head.

"You real hungry, baby?" Juicy asked.

"Damn straight…what you got for me?" as he turned his head to watch the ballgame on the television. Slowly, Juicy opened the cabinet and pulled down a big, black skillet. His eyes were glued on the fourth inning of the game as Juicy walked up on him, scaring the daylights out of him as she bashed him in the fucking head.

BAM!

BAM!

There was a fountain of blood pouring from his head. She beat him down.

He was screaming, "Mia, please stop! Please stop!"

"This is not weak ass Mia, Motherfucker. This is Juicy, Mia's Booty…and I'm going to kill you for hurting Mia!"

By this time, Robert had gone limp and was laying on the floor barely conscious, trying to figure it all out. My head started to pound again. I felt myself becoming aware of my surroundings again. I felt as though I had been out—away or both. Everything was fuzzy, but it soon began to clear and when it did, I could not believe what I was seeing or what I had done.

Robert was laid out on the kitchen floor doubled over in pain, with a frightened look on his face. I never met this Robert. This scary, little punk. Robert kept repeating over and over, "Sorry Juicy…sorry Juicy… I'll never hit you again, Juicy."

Wow!

I knew then that this person who was inside of me really did have my back. But I also knew this other person could get me locked up behind bars too. So, I helped Robert off the floor and looked at the open wound on his head, hoping it wasn't too big and that he wouldn't need stitches. But if we had to go to the hospital and they asked what happened—how could we explain that Juicy beat his ass while I was away? It sounded so crazy. I didn't even understand it myself. After I examined Robert's busted head, I realized we could make do without a doctor. So I grabbed a Band-Aid and nervously pressed it on over the cut.

Robert apologized and so did I. "I won't hit you again," he said.

And I promised him that I would never drink again, *if you know what I mean.*

We kissed, made up and became the "perfect" couple again after that night.

Robert was very attentive and began smothering me with love, but inside, I could feel myself pulling away from him. We had just been through too much.

Janiah was almost four years old and I decided it was time to do something more with my life, so I started working part-time at Mc-Donald's. I also enrolled back in school and tried to better myself while Robert stayed home selling weed to the neighbors and gang bangers. He was a part-time weed man and part-time babysitter, and since he was home all day he watched Janiah. Since we lived with his mom, she also helped.

Robert really didn't like me working because he was still ridiculously insecure, and within a few days of me working at my new job he started accusing me of flirting with the guys I was working with.

"I know you smile at them," he insisted, "you have to smile at people when you work as a cashier."

I would just shine him on and say, "Robert, please don't start this again."

But it just kept going on till it got out of hand.

One morning the devil himself came back home. It was a rainy day in December. I was walking down the street and Robert drove past me driving in his car. He slammed on the brakes and damn near ran me over as he screamed out the window, "I'm going to fuck you up bad when I get home!" shaking his fist and screaming at the top of his lungs like a mad man, "you walking like you want to be fucked!"

What?

"You switching that booty just like you begging for someone to come and fuck you!"

I just knew it was going to be some drama when I got home. I had enough of Robert and his bullshit. It was time to go. After all, I did have options. The woman who was my manager at McDonald's where I worked had taken a special interest in me. She was always trying to talk to me, but I never really let her in.

She had a gut feeling that I was in an abusive relationship, so she always told me that if I needed a place to stay, I could come to her home.

I was tired of living like this. Something had to be done and it had to be done *today*.

Not tomorrow.

Today.

When I got home, I stormed past Robert's mother, who was at home watching Janiah.

"How was your day?" Robert's mother asked following me into the bedroom.

"If you love your grandchild you won't say a word," was all I said, "I'm leaving Robert."

She didn't say a word and just left out of the room. I grabbed the phone and quickly set up the plan. It took no more than two minutes, and I started packing my bags just as quickly as I could. The plan was to have my manager pick me up in the alley in the back of the house.

But I didn't it make that far.

Robert burst through the front door and ran into the room and saw me packing.

"Bitch! You leaving me?" he screamed, "You're taking my baby!"

I didn't answer.

"I know you been fucking somebody at the job!" he shouted, "and now you and your Niggah think you're going to take my baby!"

"Robert you're crazy!" I screamed, "I'm not fucking nobody!" "I'm going to kill you bitch!" he shouted.

Just then his mother came in the room, took the baby out of the crib and walked out the door. That was her typical way of intervening.

She shut the door.

Don't see no evil.
Don't hear no evil.
Don't know no evil.

I tried to run out behind his mother but before I could get to the door Robert grabbed a bat—and bashed me in the head and the leg, both at the same time.

Bang! Bang!

And the whole world went black.

I woke up in the hospital with my head wrapped in a bandage and my leg suspended in a cast that ran all the way to my hip. I saw my family standing around my bed and they all looked distraught. But the moment I opened my eyes, NeNe and Ducky burst into tears. Ida Mae was standing at the foot of the bed with a very heavy heart.

"Why did you keep going back, Mia?" asked Ida Mae. "I knew that one day he would take you close to death."

Tears began to pour from my face. I could not speak because I was in so much pain—on the inside and the outside.

"Mom," I said trying to find a good answer to her question, "he always said sorry and told me how much he loved me." And the real truth of the matter, I always felt more sorry for him than I did for myself, but I could not fix my lips to tell my mother that.

"Well baby, it's finally over," said Ida Mae, "you and Janiah are out of here. I got you a ticket back to Chicago."

"Where is Janiah?" I asked, almost in a panic. "She's with your dad," NeNe responded.

"Where's Robert?" was my second question.

"Where he's supposed to be," said Ida, "locked the fuck up."

chapter

11

IX WEEKS LATER JANIAH AND I flew to Chicago. It was one week before my 20th birthday. I showed up humble and eager to make a new start for myself and my daughter. I also showed up with secrets. I left Robert and traded in one bad habit for another—gin. Since leaving Robert, gin and I had become real close. It was a relationship that I carried on behind closed doors. We became best friends. And when we spent time together…it was me, the gin and a ho named Juicy. She always pushed her way out and threw me in the backseat. She wanted to do all kinds of crazy shit. Look for men. Hustle them out of their money. Rob the blind lady downstairs, and spend half the night masturbating in the back room. It was this dangerous lifestyle that prompted me to buy a gun—which I always kept with me because I never knew what trouble Juicy would get me into.

Hold up, Juicy!

The only way I could control Juicy was to put the lid back on the booze.

Zip it up!

Shut it down!

And keep it away from the family.

My cousin, Erica, had invited me to move in with her. She was a beautiful young woman, about five years older than me. I had a lot of respect for Erica because she really had it all together. She had two

76

kids, a husband and a house with running water.

Her life was like a fairy tale to me. It seemed perfect, but I must confess that I also envied her a bit. She had the kind of man that didn't beat her up, so I thought he should have been awarded husband of the year.

Their life looked perfect, at least from where I had come from.

Erica mothered me. She protected me in many ways, reminding me of my Aunt Mary. She saw the beauty in me that I could not see in myself and always tried to bring out the best in me.

Once I left Robert, I began to get some clarity about my life. Once he stopped throwing punches, I could see straight. I only wanted one thing out of life… that my little girl Janiah didn't grow up to be anything like me. I didn't want her to go through all the trials and tribulations I had to endure. My mission was to get myself together and get my daughter into the best school and make sure she got all the love a little girl can get. Eventually, I went back to high school and graduated and checked into attending a local junior college. I took the bus back and forth to school each day, and found myself very attracted to the bus driver.

Who was this beautiful man?

I hadn't found myself attracted to anyone since Robert, but I must admit that I was intrigued by this quiet, gentle spirit. He was the opposite of Robert. It didn't hurt that he was fine, too. Fine as hell, I might add. He was always helping me find my way to and from wherever I was supposed to be going. I felt safe with him. How could I not? I learned early on in our friendship that he was a black belt in karate. I would later come to find out that his name was Terry and his family owned the bus company that provided the transportation for the school.

Terry always invited me to go for dinner and I would always say no. But one day, I gave in and said, "Yes."

I knew that night at dinner, I really liked him. I wasn't thrilled about dating again, but I saw that Terry was so different, so I let my guard down a bit. But that didn't include sex—no sex for six months. That would give me an opportunity to see if he was interested in me or if he was like everyone else and only wanted Juicy. "I respect that," he said without question.

I could see that he was confident and secure with himself, unlike Robert.

Over the next few months I got to know more about him and his childhood. He came from a wonderful family. They reminded me of the Cosby's, but their last name was Smith. They lived in a little city just outside of Chicago called Harvey.

The Smiths were a very well-to-do and popular family. They were functional, not dysfunctional. It was refreshing to see Black people in this light. The matriarch of the family, Sandra Smith, was the perfect mom. She was the kind of mother you dreamt about. She lived and breathed for her kids, and always took a strong interest in all of their friends. So, no wonder I was nervous when Terry asked me and Janiah to his house for dinner.

I accepted his invitation and despite my nerves, it was a wonderful night. Sandra really took to me and we became very, very close. I was so comfortable with her. I opened up about the abuse I had gone through and she felt compelled to help me. She also knew that I was living in my cousin's house in tight quarters. Sandra stepped in like the fairy godmother and made some magic happen. She put Janiah and I in our own apartment and even paid for Janiah's medical bills when she got sick. She also got me a gig at her family's car lot.

Terry and his family were just what I needed to get my confidence back because I had lost every ounce of it. I began to feel a sense of direction and purpose again in my life again, though I did suffer from serious blows with depression. The wounds that Robert inflicted ran deep, and his absence did not take the pain away.

It was still there.

It was there right in front of me—staring at me—everyday.

I called her *Janiah*.

So, I drank when no one looked, and sometimes I drank when people did look but I always disguised it as "social" drinking. I never went without, whether the booze came from the bar or the bottom of my purse, but like I said I never went without.

Late at night, I would lock myself in the bathroom and drink myself into oblivion. Juicy came in and took over every time. She would play with me—rub on my breasts, booty and in between my legs.

Go get us a Niggah, Bitch!

We need someone ELSE to play!

I would sit on her big ass to keep her quiet.

I didn't want her to wake the neighbors, and I couldn't afford to introduce Terry to Juicy.

The daytime hours were much better. I could finally give some thought to what I wanted to do with my life. I had always dreamt about becoming a lawyer. It seemed like such an important job because I always hated how people always judged others without evidence or facts. I could defend the innocent or the wrongly accused. It made sense to me. Hell, people had always "judged" me. It seemed that for the first time everything was right on track.

I was dating a gorgeous man who had done so much to boost my self esteem. Terry was in love with my body and always complimented me. He didn't trip out when guys looked at my body. He just wanted them to respect me. And sometimes, he had to be my defender when things got out of line. And sometimes things did get out of line, more on that later. It was during this time that I also began to see myself differently, and for the first time I started to see what everyone else saw when they looked at me. I really liked my booty. It was very nice and round, but even so, I still couldn't make out why so many guys were going crazy over my booty, especially Terry. My booty was his favorite part.

We were having a ball together and growing closer by the minute. Things were going well, but deep down inside, I felt like I was waiting for something to change. It seemed too perfect. On the other side of my good times, I was filled with my own form of insecurities. The haunting echoes of my past began to sing to me again.

Would Terry grow tired of defending my honor?

79

Would my booty get in the way of Terry's love for me?

One hot summer night, Terry and I were out at this very popular club in Harvey. We were having a great time—dancing and partying. "You want something to drink baby?" he asked. I paused.

No, I froze in my tracks.

Terrified.

A drink?

Booze?

Liquor?

"What's wrong, baby?" asked Terry, noticing the frozen reflection on my face.

"Nothing," I said trying to calm my nerves. I couldn't blow this one. Terry was the perfect boyfriend. I couldn't lose myself in the booze and let Juicy out without supervision. But how could I explain this to Terry?

He'd never understand. He would leave me and I would be alone again.

"Let me get you a drink," he insisted.

"Okay," I said, dying to take that drink. Truth be told, I was licking my lips inside.

Terry handed me a drink, and I took a swig. Much to my surprise and delight, it was one of my favorite companions, Vodka. I swallowed that drink so fast that I wanted to throw it up—lest Terry take one good look at me and realize that I had a problem. I did have a problem, but Terry didn't have to know that.

"Do you want another?" he asked.

"No," I said excusing myself to the bathroom. It was time to dig deep, deep in the bottom of the purse. I wanted it bad, another drink. I knew that drinking had a side effect, and in my case that affect would be called Juicy. But I couldn't fight this urgency to take a drink. Like I said before, I had a thing. I didn't say it was a 'pretty' thing, just a thing. In other words, I didn't give a damn.

I got wasted in the stall and I came out brand new. You could have taken me for somebody else.

My head started to pound and I could feel myself getting dizzy and disoriented. I stumbled my way back to the dance floor and met up with Terry. At once, he noticed the change in me.

"What's wrong, baby?" he asked.

"Just a little headache," I said feeling on my forehead which was starting to throb and pound. I could feel myself slipping away as Juicy emerged and began to take control of things. Within seconds, I could feel my body temperature rise. It was as if I had a pulse between my legs and it began to beat to the sound of its own drum. It pumped to the rhythm of hot and horny.

Hot and horny.

Hot and horny.

"Come with me to the restroom!" Juicy commanded Terry. "Again?" he asked, puzzled. "I thought you just went."

"It's time to go back," Juicy insisted. "I got something for you." "In the restroom?" he asked.

Juicy didn't have time to debate the topic of bathroom visits with Terry on the dance floor, so she just grabbed his hand and pulled him into the women's restroom, which surprisingly was empty. After a quick survey of the joint, Juicy kicked one of the stall doors in with her foot and pulled Terry in behind her.

Terry watched in disbelief as Juicy put the top down on the toilet and sat down on it, turning her hungry eyes to Terry's crotch area. She unzipped his pants like a hungry savage in expectation of a full blown feast.

"Mia?" asked Terry.

Juicy locked eyes with Terry just before pulling out his hefty-sized package, and almost swallowing it whole she began to suck.

"Mia ain't here. Say hello to Juicy!"

"Whoa!" said Terry in a state of sexual surrender. Juicy was working it out. She was sucking and swallowing, pulling Terry's dick forward, then back and up to the front again. The visual alone was worth catching on Candid Camera, as Juicy was on her way to winning the Blow Job of the Year Award.

The stall was banging—in a very literal sense of the word with Terry ramming back and forth. They were so involved in the "business at hand" neither one realized that a stranger had walked in, and was listening intently from the other side of the door.

"What the hell?" asked a woman's voice on the other side of the door. "Hey Bitch!" screamed Juicy, "come on in here and get some of this good dick!"

"What?" asked the woman in shock.

"It's your night, baby…" Juicy said to Terry, "get two Bitches for the price of one!"

And with that the woman gasped and quickly rushed from the bathroom.

Terry couldn't help but laugh, but Juicy didn't break character. She was in it to win it—and nothing was going to distract her from that tasty dick. It didn't take Terry long to fall back into his part either. Within seconds of the woman leaving, Terry began moaning, grinding, rocking and withering. He was holding Juicy's head in between his hands as she sucked all the juice out of the berry and Terry literally exploded all over Juicy's face.

"Cummmmminnnggg…." was all he could manage to squeeze from his vocal chords in between the pants and moans.

Juicy's face was filled with creamy white as she sat back and slowly licked her lips.

Terry was speechless.

By then, there were several women entering the restroom. Once Terry *came*—he came back to himself and realized this whole scene was risky. He knew they could get thrown out of the club for carrying on like this. Terry was a conservative gentleman at heart, and this porn show was a little out of his comfort zone.

Juicy wanted to go at it again right there on the spot, but Terry stopped her saying, "We gotta go!" And with that he opened the stall door, peeked around the corner and when the coast was clear he bolted out of the bathroom, leaving Juicy behind to clean herself up.

So Juicy left too. They went straight to the car and Juicy was ready for round two. She ripped his pant offs and jumped on top of his dick. She could not stop fucking him until he came all up inside of her.

"Wow Mia!" said Terry out of breath, "you are a real freak!" "Niggah," snapped Juicy, "I told you to call me Juicy."

"You're nothing like that shy girl I met on the bus," he said with a grin, "you've been hiding, Juicy."

Terry started up the car and began to drive them back home. Juicy was "eyeing" Terry, checking out his watch and his wallet— which was almost falling out of his pocket. She thought about charging him *and* robbing him, but, she also knew that Terry was a decent guy for Mia— and she didn't want to blow it for Mia yet. Juicy leaned her head back on the seat and began to feel the familiar headache that she was so accustomed to feeling.

"Damnit," she mumbled.

"What's wrong, baby?" asked Terry.

"The Bitch is coming back," she said before slipping away. "Juicy, you okay?" asked Terry.

Juicy, said Mia to herself shaking her head. Once Mia regained full awareness, she saw that her clothes were off and she was horribly embarrassed. She also saw Terry's zipper open and the side of his dick was pushing out. She shook her head a second time, before finally getting the nerve up to ask, "What did I do?"

Terry just laughed and said, "You did exactly what I wanted you to do..."

"That wasn't me," I said in my defense, "I was drinking." "Yeah," said Terry laughing, "blame it on the Vodka. I don't care who you blame...just please do that again."

Oh damn, Mia thought. This has gone haywire. Now Terry was crazy about me—I mean Juicy. But I couldn't afford to tell him the truth. He would think I was crazy. Why wouldn't he? At this point, I was beginning to think I was crazy too. Juicy was getting stronger, and her visits were staying longer. I was blacking out and didn't remember a thing.

Oh God.

This could be a problem.

Would Terry like me—now that he had been introduced to Juicy?

I was too afraid to find out, so I continued drinking and Juicy kept coming out to play. Actually, I felt inadequate to satisfy Terry without Juicy. In other words, I became as dependent on Juicy as I was on the alcohol.

Two masters.

One slave.

My insecurities began to grow and I started to accept what most people felt—that the booty was more important than me. And it was here that I began to disappear in my relationships.

Terry was always giving 'Juicy' such glowing "reviews" how could I ever let him meet Mia again? Though Terry did enjoy "Mia" outside of the bedroom, so much in fact that he asked me to be his "girlfriend."

I accepted and Terry and I became inseparable. We went everywhere together. He loved my little Janiah. Terry would always comment that "Janiah was as beautiful as her mommy" but I hated to hear that, because I didn't want her to be anything like me, especially in the "booty department."

Things between Terry and I were pretty good but we started to run into some bumps in the road. One night Terry and I went out to the movies, and there were three rough-looking, thuggish guys just hanging out with nothing better to do than gawk and point at girls.

Hey baby…what's your name?

Come over here and let me rub on that ass.

Damn.

Look at the tits on that Bitch!

I knew there was going to be some drama at the movies tonight. These guys were talking smack to every girl who crossed their path, and as we approached, the guys turned all of their attention to Terry.

Hey dude.

Damn, they said looking at me. Is that your woman?

I know you be tapping that ass.

What you feeding that big cornbread eating bitch?

Man, that's the biggest booty I ever seen in my life.

Is the bitch pregnant from the back?

Where you from, baby? The ATL?

You ever dance at the Magic City?

Terry's face turned blistering red and I could see he was about to lose it.

"Hey man…" said Terry in a sharp voice, "don't disrespect the lady, man….especially my lady."

They just laughed and kept on talking.

Hey man…can we share that ass?

She got enough ass for all us.

Brother, you can't handle all that by yourself.

That was it. Terry had enough. Without saying so much as a word to me, he let go of my hand and pushed through the crowd to the loud-talking, ignorant guys and got right in their way.

"Man, apologize to my woman!" he demanded.

"Niggah," said the ring leader, "get the fuck out of our face before we fuck you up and fuck your woman."

There were no more words after that. The only sound effect was Terry's foot smashing into one guy's nose and his fist going into another guy's groin area. Much to their surprise, Terry was demonstrating his skills in martial arts. He was a black belt, remember?

Ouch!

Ouch!

It was going down. These guys were getting their ass whooped. This was a real beat down. I noticed out of the corner of my eye that one of their partners was making his way up the sidewalk, digging in his jacket and pulling out a metal object.

Oh damn! I thought to myself. I hope that wasn't what I thought it was. I started getting really scared. This was getting really out of hand.

The guy pulled out a gun and started to hold it up in the air and let off a shot. The blasting sound of the bullet ricocheted off a nearby wall and the crowd went nuts. People started running and screaming. Within moments sirens were blasting from every direction. The thugs went one way and we went another.

I ran and grabbed Terry and we took off in the direction of the car, bobbing and weaving in between the panicked crowd. Once we got in the car I broke down into tears. I could not stop crying. Terry could have been killed tonight. One shot in the wrong direction and it could have been all over. It was all because of this damn booty.

Why?

Why me?

Why did God give me this booty?

Why did I have to go through so much pain?

Why do people look at this booty and judge me?

I was beginning to feel like the African lady, Sara. I felt as though I was nothing more than a freak on display. To make matters worse, Terry wanted to have a little "talk."

"Baby," he said taking my hand, "I need to talk to you."

Uh oh, I thought. *Here it comes.*

"I want to see you and I still want to be with you," he started out saying, "but not in public."

I wanted to burst into tears. I couldn't believe that Terry was shutting it down like that.

No more dinners?

Movies?

Dancing in the club?

"What?" I asked.

"We can still hang out at home…" said Terry, "and drink."

I was not feeling that. I knew right then and there that this would change the whole relationship. I had never felt so rejected in my life.

"So," I said defensively, "you want to cut off our public life but you want to keep the private life?"

"Not necessarily in that way," he tried to defend.

"Well, how about this then…" I said, "you want to kill the dating scene but you want to keep the bedroom scenes?"

Terry didn't respond. He just looked away and lowered his head.

"Baby, I hate to say this…" he said. "What?"

"You're dangerous," said Terry, "you're going to get a brother killed with all that ass."

"What happened to your black belt?" I asked getting more and more angry. "Are you scared?"

"It's just not worth it," he said.

Worth it? I thought to myself.

He doesn't think I'm worth it.

But he thinks JUICY is worth it. He'll hide me in public but he wants to play with her in private.

In that moment, I began to dislike Terry—almost as much as I had come to dislike myself. The hurt was on 'public display' all over my face.

"Baby, I love you," he said, "and I don't want to change you but I can't handle the attention your booty brings."

"So what do you want me to do, Terry?" I asked, "you want me to buy some Moo Moos?"

He didn't answer but then again he didn't have to.

I didn't think, I said to myself disgusted, *if I took to wearing Moo Moos, then I would no longer be your show piece.*

"We're coming to the end, aren't we?" I asked, straight out. Again, he didn't answer.

"Baby," he said urgently, "I still want to be with you…"

No quicker than I could feel joy at this declaration did he smash my beating heart by adding the end to that sentence—*in the house.*

"I still want to be with you in the house," he repeated.

"Yeah right," I mumbled beneath my breath.

There was a long pause and I knew that Terry could easily cut it off with me, but he couldn't cut it off with Juicy. He was as dependent on Juicy as I was.

Damn.

This was deep.

Who was Juicy? She had a magnetic attraction and men were called to her like crack heads are called to the pipe. This was a "crack addition" all right—men were called to the "crack" of my ass and it overshadowed the rest of me.

"It's over," I said. "Take me home."

He wanted to say something, but I gently placed one finger over his 'moving' lips. Silence, I gestured.

Just be quiet.

That was the last time I ever saw Terry. He could never live within my world and I no longer felt welcome inside of his. I was so distraught after our break-up that I spent about three days drunk off my ass. Ironically, the only comforter I would have in my time of need would be Juicy.

chapter

12

*A*FTER TERRY AND I BROKE up everything looked different. Not only did I break up with Terry but I had to break up with his family too. And life in Harvey would never be the same. I felt like a stranger in this town, as my cousin Erica and I had already drifted apart slowly after my arrival.

Terry had given me some of myself back. But it was a "temporary fix" at best because the moment Terry left—my confidence blew out the back window—and me and Janiah were headed back to Los Angeles to Ida Mae and my family.

On my way back home, I couldn't help but reflect upon my time in Harvey. In many ways, Harvey had been good to me but I was tormented by a string of unanswered questions.

Should I just let Juicy take over?

Would that end the pain?

After all, Juicy did ask me to let her lead. She promised me that she would give me the best life I could ever dream of—but only if I listened to her. But I never wanted to be just a "booty." That's what everybody wanted me to be, but I couldn't consent to playing that part.

When I arrived back in Los Angeles I moved back in with my family. I had been gone so long that everything looked different but nothing had really changed. That was a tough adjustment because I hadn't lived with them for more than ten years.

Years later, Ida Mae finally hit the jackpot with two "golden eggs." The golden eggs were her two illegitimate sons, Bobby and Levi. Ironically, when their biological father died he left them enough money in his will to start their own business. Like father like son, they opened up gas stations in the greater Los Angeles area.

Ida Mae finally got her wish—real gas stations with working pumps. So, of course, the moment I stepped foot on California soil they had me working in the back office using my computer skills. It wasn't a glamorous occupation but the income helped while I took real estate classes on the side.

Janiah and I both needed space or "extra air" because Ida Mae was always on my back trying to sell me off to the next customer that pulled up in the gas station. Actually, it was a stressful time for both Janiah and I. She had hit the teenage years and was going through her teenage transformation. She was so intelligent and had high aspirations of being a lawyer. She needed a quiet place to study without Ida Mae's ridiculous commentary in the background. And I, too, needed room to stretch out. So obviously, this was a temporary situation.

Ida Mae hadn't changed a bit. She was still the same old Ida Mae, and all she wanted was some money. Ida couldn't understand how I could not be rich by now. She thought my body should have earned me some high dollar wages.

"Bitch…you still broke?" was all Ida kept asking me. Every time she would look at me she would shake her head. "What the fuck?" she said, "I can't believe your ass came back here with no money."

"Mom," I said in my defense, "I did come back with a certificate in data entry."

"A data what, Bitch?"

"Computers mom," I said. "I'm using my computer skills to help the boys at the gas station."

"Fuck that," said Ida. "You can get a great paying job with that big ass you got!"

On the edge of Ida's comment, daddy walked in and added his two cents. "Baby, I've got a good friend that I want you to meet."

Oh damn, I thought to myself.

"If that doesn't work out, I got somebody for her to meet, too," said Ida.

Damn, I said again.

How could both of your parents want to sell your ass?

I definitely can't let them meet Juicy.

The three of them would become best friends.

Two days later, Ida Mae tried to set me up with a rich guy named Ray. She invited him over to the house one morning after breakfast.

He landed on our doorstep with a big grin and a wad of cash. She had been raffling me off like a mail order bride for about two years showing off every picture I had ever taken.

Dang Momma.

I don't even know this guy.

I'm not the least bit attracted to him, I said to Ida Mae, pulling her aside in the kitchen.

She could have blown her stack when I told her.

"You don't have to like him!" she said in a sharp tone, "Just fuck him, Mia, so he can give us...oh, I mean *you* some of that money."

"Mom," I said, "I don't like him like that."

"If your baby girl needed to eat and you had this Niggah waiving thousands at you... you telling me you would let your baby starve before you would go and fuck him."

"Huh?" I asked, caught off guard by Ida's question. "Thousands of opportunities are passing you by," she said, "and here you sit...starving." And she looked at me and said, "you are a dumb bitch. If I could be you for one day, I would show you how to make money with that ass."

But she wasn't me, and it wasn't going down like that today. Ida had to go back into the other room and tell Ray to "go home." It was a hurtful thing to watch Ida whisper to Ray, "Don't worry...I'll set you up with her. It's just going to take a little longer than I thought." I was hurt by Ida's attempt to sell me off like cattle in a field, but I knew what I was getting myself into coming back to her house.

I started to ask myself, "Do I have a problem because I don't like fucking for money?"

It didn't feel natural to me.

Everybody noticed the "money machine" but me.

Like I said, it didn't feel natural. But I felt tortured and caught between being broke and being moral—especially under the weight of Ida's promise that "no man would ever love me. And that they would only want to use me for what I had and for what I could do for them."

Needless to say, my self-esteem couldn't take the constant jabs from Ida. She was poking holes in my soul. From time to time, I would go on dates with guys I liked, and when I would come home and go the fridge to grab a bite to eat, Ida was standing over my shoulder offering her two, unwelcomed cents again.

"Bitch," she started out, "I know you ain't hungry!" "What?" I asked.

"And I know you brought some money home for me and the baby" she stuttered, "I mean the baby."

She pushed the issue every time I went on a date. I could never just have a friend. Ida always insisted that they "pay" me and if they didn't something was "terribly wrong" in her opinion. Eventually, I knew I would have to give up the booty and let Ida pimp me or move out.

I opted for the move. It was easier on my nerves. So, I moved in with my older sister, NeNe. She loved me so much. She did not get into my business. NeNe never pressured nor judged me for not selling my ass. She didn't try to pimp me, but she definitely appreciated my body. She always wanted a booty like mine. All NeNe liked to do was party and smoke weed. When I moved in, I became her party partner.

One night NeNe and I went to this club and so many guys were on us. NeNe started to curse at them and say, "get off of her ass…if you want some ass look at this one." She raised her dress up and showed them the crack of her ass. Every time NeNe got drunk she would get naked and talk shit.

I was drinking that night too. In truth, I was still drinking every chance I got, and it wouldn't take long before the familiar headache would come on. I began to notice that not only did Juicy stay longer, but she came out quicker. It seemed like in one swallow I was gone. Juicy was seizing the moment—her eyes would scout the room for every bit of cash, diamonds, gold and tin. Juicy was on it. She had laser like vision and since she sat low—she was always scanning the size of "bulges" looking for two kinds of bulges—a fat wallet and a big dick.

She spotted one. He had two big bulges—so he was the one she was interested in. She stood up and walked by him, and that was all it really ever took. Once they honed in on Juicy they were hooked.

No turning back.

"Hey Baby!" Juicy called out. "Come over here."

Before Juicy could get the words out, the guy was already in her face and Juicy liked what she was seeing. He was sexy with a rock hard body and eyes that were penetrating. The guy's eyes were hazel and his skin was a beautiful tan color. It was nice that he was fine, but Juicy didn't care about the looks—her main concern was the wallet with the dick being a close second.

"What's your name?" asked Juicy.

"Mr. Big," he replied, trying to look real cool. "Why do they call you Mr. Big?" Juicy asked. He just looked down and smiled.

"Why do they call you Juicy?" he asked. Juicy turned around and smiled.

He smiled too. He understood and she understood. So now that we have this great understanding, *let's get to it*—Juicy thought. He was thinking about fucking her and she was thinking about fucking him up. The agreement was the same but at the same time different.

So there was no protest when Mr. Big took my hand and we started heading toward the door. Out of the corner of Juicy's eye, she saw NeNe trying to make eye contact and figure out what was going on, but Juicy didn't have time to do any explaining. She would leave that for Mia to do later.

Mr. Big led Juicy to an over-sized Mercedes with shiny rims.

Nice, Juicy thought to herself, before sliding inside on the passenger's side. Mr. Big hopped in the driver's side and it was on and popping. Juicy started rubbing Mr. Big's dick and all of a sudden he became "Mr. Bigger."

"That's why they call you Mr. Big," said Juicy. He laughed.

He was feeling all over Juicy's ass and that's when Juicy started to get really turned on. She wanted to fuck him so bad. He put his finger up Juicy's dress and it was soaking wet.

"You got a rubber?" he asked.

"No," said Juicy, "I don't need no rubbers."

"I got a box in the car," he insisted, and so we headed that way. Once we got there, all he could talk about was how bad he wanted to fuck me because Juicy drove him crazy.

"Well," said Juicy, "we can fuck but you gotta give me two thousand dollars!"

And he paid it!

It was short and sweet.

He came in under two minutes.

All in a day's work thought Juicy as she counted that money and scoped the car out for valuables. She saw a ring with diamonds sitting on the dashboard, and she smooth leaned over and swooped it up without missing a beat by distracting Mr. Big with extra kisses to the cheek. That gave her enough time to drop the jewelry in her purse and keep it moving.

"I'll ride you again someday," she said, opening the door to jump out. When her foot hit the concrete, her head began to spin and throb. *Uh oh,* Juicy thought to herself, *the bitch is coming back.* And with that, Juicy fell back against the front seat.

"Shit!" Juicy shouted.

"What's wrong?" asked Mr. Big, leaning into her.

"Bitch is coming back," mumbled Juicy before almost going unconscious. Two seconds later, Mia opens her eyes only to see Mr. Big staring her down—with his big body almost smothering her.

"What, bitch?" he asked. Dazed, Mia pushes him off her.

"Bitch!" she screamed, "who are you and why are you calling me a bitch?"

Mr. Big was confused. He pulled back, "I'm not calling you a bitch…you're the one that just said something about the bitch coming back."

"Oh shit," said Mia to herself, "Juicy was here."

Filled with embarrassment and uncertainty about her "shady" behavior, Mia could only wonder what happened. In that moment, Mia didn't have the heart to ask the obvious questions.

1. Who are you?

2. What did I just do?

If Juicy was involved (and she always was), Mia was certain it involved trickery, sex, blowjobs, liquor, thievery and money. These were Juicy's primary personality traits. And as Mia opened her purse, there sat the evidence of an evening out on the town with Juicy— alcohol on the breath, sore mouth from sucking so hard, sore pussy from fucking so hard and a purse full of money and a big diamond ring.

"So when can I see you again?" he asked with a big grin on his face, "you're the sexiest freak I ever had." "What?" she asked with her lip turned up, frowning.

"I never knew any woman who swallowed like that!" he insisted.

Oh my God, Mia thought to herself.

"It was like you were gargling my shit!" he said with a laugh. Between the booze and the story, Mia was ready to throw up.

She was nauseous and couldn't believe what she was hearing. "That's not me," Mia defended angrily.

"Whoever that was…can I take her out again?" he asked. "You will never see her again!" said Mia, "you filthy pig!" "What?" he asked confused by the sudden 'switch.' "You're a fucking CRAZY bitch!"

"Stop this car and let me out!" demanded Mia.

"Get your crazy ass out of my car!" he said, slamming on the brakes. "And you ARE the bitch that you said was coming back!

Mia was so outdone…as she jumped from the car so fast she landed on her knees on the concrete.

But there was no compassion from Mr. Big—he just laughed at her and sped off.

Thankfully, Mia was not hurt and was only blocks away from her sister NeNe's house. The walk was long and painful as she recounted the unpleasant events of the evening. She knew that something had to be done but she didn't know where to start. She was in too deep and there was no way to return the money or the valuables. The best she could do was throw it in a shoe box that she had labeled Janiah's college fund. That made it easier to swallow (no pun intended) without choking on it.

Mia also knew it was time to get help—*real* help. When all fails, call on God.

The next day Mia walked into the church of Rev. Leon, the local minister at the 85th Chapel of the Holy Trinity Church of God. Distraught, she took a seat in the front pew and began to weep, and cry out to God. It seemed as though within moments, she was answered when she looked up into the kind, loving eyes of Reverend Leon, a conservative-looking minister, dressed in a black and white robe with sacred symbols and a big, gold cross dangling from the center of his chest. He wore black, rimmed glasses and bore a gentle smile that matched his gentle spirit.

"Sweet child," he said calmly, "what's the matter?"

"I have a devil living inside of me," was all that Mia could utter between her tears and sobs.

"Child…" he said, "You are a child of God. Why do you say such things about yourself?"

"I am a child of God," she told the reverend, "but there's someone else who lives inside of me…and the way I see it…she's best friends with the devil."

The reverend looked a bit confused, but listened intently as Mia continued.

"It all started when I was 15," said Mia. "I took a drink of spiked punch…and I started hearing voices."

"Voices?" he asked concerned. "Tell me more about the voices." "It was the voice of Juicy," said Mia, barely able to hold herself together.

"The voice of Juicy?" he asked, taking a seat beside her. "Who's Juicy, sweet child?"

"Juicy is my booty," said Mia matter-of-factly, as Mia stood up and turned around, introducing the reverend to Juicy. The Reverend's eyes almost popped out of his head!

Holy Mother of God, said the Reverend, trying to conceal the obvious erection that was bulging beneath his robe.

"See Reverend…" said Mia, "this is my biggest problem."

The reverend nodded and wiped the sweat from his brow, in between beats of staring at her ass.

"Come child," he said, trying to gather himself, "sit down." Mia sat again.

He took a deep breath once she sat down.

"Juicy only comes out when I drink…" explained Mia. "Juicy likes gin and vodka."

The reverend's brow raised.

"When Juicy comes out, she takes total control of my body…"

"What do you mean?" he asked.

"It's hard to explain…Juicy loves sex…money…and men…" The reverend was on the edge of his seat—listening intently as Mia attempted to explain the unexplainable. So, he interrupted her with a question.

"Can you show me?" he asked.

"What?" asked Mia, stopping in her tracks.

"I want to meet Juicy," said the Reverend. "I want to introduce her to the Lord."

A giant pause filled the room with a deafening silence.

"I need to meet this Juicy," said the Reverend.

"It's the only way to free you."

"She only comes out when I have gin," said Mia.

"What about red wine?" he asked with a raised brow.

"No!" insisted Mia, "you can't meet Juicy! I need help, Reverend!"

"I know child…I'm trying to help you now!" he insisted.

"I can't, Reverend!" screamed Mia, as she jumped up and ran out the front door of the church, with the Reverend running behind her with a communion cup filled with red wine, pouring over the top.

"Juicy come back!" screamed the Reverend.

Juicy!

Juicy!

chapter

13

THAT DAY IN THE CHURCH was my darkest hour. I realized that no man could ever solve or understand my problem, whether he was a minister or a con man. Truthfully, they were one and the same. They all wanted a piece of Juicy, but I just wanted to be free. It had been almost thirteen years that I had been dealing with this split personality, and just weeks away from my 28th birthday, I knew something had to give. Me or my sanity, but something had to give.

Me or my sanity, but something had to give.

I'm not what people think I am—but *I* am what people think I am. I also realized that every morning when I woke up I wanted a drink. No, I needed a drink to get me through the day, and then I needed another drink to get me through the night, but that was only so I could make it to the morning and get another drink. Was it me that wanted the drink or was it Juicy who forced me to surrender myself so she could come out? Either way, I had to drink.

It was a problem and I needed somebody, somewhere to fix it. So, I got out the Yellow Pages and started searching for the closest rehab center in the neighborhood. Maybe there I could connect to some *other* crazy people who could help me. Perhaps there were even others out there like me.

❧

The room was sterile-looking with several rickety chairs set up in a circle. There were a lot of people in the room, but I couldn't tell right off the bat if any of them were just like me. There was a plain looking woman sitting in the middle of the floor. I guess she was the speaker. In fact she was because she was the only one speaking.

"Welcome," she said quietly as she went around the room offering each of us the opportunity to introduce ourselves. But I didn't like their introduction because everyone who stood up said their name out loud followed by a proud announcement, "I'm an alcoholic."

But when it came my turn to stand up, I stood up and said, "Hi... my name is Mia."

Hi *Mia*, the room blurted out.

"And I'm happy to be here," I stuttered.

They nodded and smiled, but it was as if they were waiting for more.

"This is my first meeting," I added. Again, they nodded and smiled.

"Thank you for having me," I said rapidly and sat right back down.

Obviously, I wasn't into heavy confession. I didn't know if I was an alcoholic, and I didn't feel like I needed to admit to anything I was uncertain of—and at this point, I was uncertain.

The meeting was uneventful to me for the most part. I didn't feel that I really connected to most of the people there—they all looked strange. And I wasn't feeling like telling the whole room about my problem with the talking booty. I didn't want to be the joke of the room. They had problems with booze—I had problems with the booty and the booze. Hell, maybe I was an alcoholic, but just didn't feel like saying it out loud today—maybe tomorrow.

Or the next.

As I stared around the room, I noticed that most of the people were worn like old shoes. Their skin looked like old, beat-up leather. It was weathered and torn. I even noticed that there was a scent that came out of their pores. It was like a breathing hangover. They reeked of alcohol from the inside out. But I did notice someone who was very different, unique...downright exotic. She was beautiful, so beautiful was she that I could not help but to stare. Not in a sexual way, of course, but just in an admiring way. She had bronze skin with deep auburn-colored hair and piercing hazel eyes.

What? I thought to myself. I couldn't imagine her being an alcoholic, but sure enough when her turn came, she stood up and said, "Hi…my name is Argentina and I'm an alcoholic."

Wow.

She was an alcoholic?

I guess you can't judge beauty by its cover.

I couldn't help but notice as I stared at her—that she also stared back. We were both drawn into each other's eyes. It seemed like she was judging me as much as I was judging her. Neither of us belonged but still somehow we both fit. At the end of the meeting, we naturally gravitated towards one another and "small talk" began. "Hi…" she said extending a hand.

"Hi," I responded in kind.

She smiled at me with such warmth that I immediately embraced her. I couldn't stop staring at her—how could someone be so beautiful and be an alcoholic?

"For the life of me," I said, "I can't see why you're here." "I feel the same way about you," she quickly inserted. "If you only knew," I said rolling my eyes. "I got issues." "Me too," she said laughing out loud.

"Your body is so beautiful," she said in quiet observation. "Your face is so unique," I offered in exchange.

"Wish I had that butt," she said laughing.

"No you don't…" I warned her, but just left it at that. "You wanna grab a bite?" she asked.

"Sure," I eagerly accepted.

"I live just around the corner," she said. "Come to my house and I'll make us some sandwiches."

It seemed like within minutes of meeting her, I was sitting in this beautiful woman's home. I would come to learn that Argentina was a hard core alcoholic who drank to cover up the pain of growing up with a father who was a molester. "It's so hard to believe that you were in that meeting today," I confessed. "You're so beautiful to me…"

"I hate when people call me beautiful," she said, "my father used to say that every time he raped me."

"Oh my God," I said, "I'm so sorry…and I thought I had the crazy family. Just like you hate people calling you beautiful…I hate people thinking I should be a whore because of my body."

"What's the deal with your family?" she asked. "They all think I should use my body to get paid." "What does that mean?" she inquired.

"They expect me to be a ho, a stripper or whatever it takes to get paid."

"Damn…" she said quietly.

"My sister told me I was a wasted product of God…and that he had given me this body to get paid."

We both sat in silence for a long time. No one said a word.

Not her. Not me.

It was like we were both brooding in silence over some destiny that was claiming us that neither of us wanted.

"I like being here with you," she said to me. "You feel safe." "I like you too," I said.

"Where do we go from here?" she asked.

Silence.

Silence.

And still more silence.

"You want to have a drink?" I asked her with a laugh. "I know you don't have any booze in here."

"You might be surprised," she said moving towards a locked cabinet. "I keep a little stash for the nights when I'm plagued by nightmares."

She opened the locked cabinet and it looked like the corner liquor store.

What the hell?

She had every kind of alcohol on the market, legal and illegal. It was unbelievable—that this beautiful woman, who had just been to an AA meeting, had enough booze in her house to supply the whole city in case of a shortage.

"Wait…wait…" I said holding up my hand in protest, "how long have you been sober?"

"Well," she said with a grin, "I've been going to meetings for five years…I haven't gotten sober yet."

On that note, we burst out laughing. It was tragic, but yet at the same time, it was funny.

Who would have ever thought? You never know how life is going to present itself and you can never judge the package that it comes in.

Argentina pulled out two bottles and two glasses.

Two bottles?

Two glasses?

Vodka.

And gin.

Me and her.

Uh oh.

I didn't touch the stuff—at first. I let Argentina do the drinking and I did the talking.

"You don't want a drink?" she asked, noticing that my glass went untouched.

I shook my head as I stared down the drink.

"Come on," begged Argentina, "I don't like to drink alone." "I'm scared to drink," I said.

"Why?" she asked, "you don't like being an alcoholic?"

"I have a kid," I confessed, "and I don't want to lose her because of the drinking. She's a good kid…she wants to be a lawyer."

"How old is your kid?" "Fifteen," I said.

"I can't imagine having a kid," said Argentina, "I can barely take care of myself."

"It's tough with no help…" I said, "really tough."

The more I thought about how hard it was the more I wanted a drink.

Two drinks maybe.

"Girl, pour me a drink," I said. "Thought you'd never ask," said Argentina, overly excited that I was going to be drinking with her.

Only if she really knew who was going to be drinking with us.

She would really be excited.

A few drinks into it—I could see another whole side of Argentina coming out. It was almost as if she had a "Juicy" locked inside of her too. She was getting super touchy feely with me.

"Relax baby," she kept whispering, "are you hot?"

"No," I was thinking to myself, "you have the air conditioning on, don't you?"

"I'm getting hot," said Argentina taking off her shirt and pants, which left her sitting in her panties and bras. This made me nervous and I started downing the whole damn bottle.

"Easy baby," said Argentina laughing, "save some for the drunks on the block."

I laughed.

She was funny. Damn.

Here comes the headache. I almost wanted to stop it, but it was too late. I felt Juicy waking up and I started getting sleepy— real sleepy. Within minutes, I was stone, cold out.

And here's Juicy….

"Damn those titties look sweet and perky!" said Juicy, "what is your name you fine mother fucker!"

"You know my name, Mia," said Argentina. "My name ain't Mia… I'm Juicy."

"Juicy?" said Argentina with big eyes.

"That scary, dumb bitch is on vacation!" said Juicy. "I wish she would stay gone…so I could run this world the way I want to run this world and make this money for that broke bitch!"

"What?" asked Argentina, laughing.

"All this ass I got on me…" said Juicy, "this Bitch could be rich now!"

"Wow…" said Argentina, "you act a little different when you drink."

"Shit…" said Juicy under her breath, "I act like me all the time… drunk or not! I'm a stone freak. A stone ho. A stone gangsta…

a stone bitch…"

"Damn," said Argentina, "you just stone…stone…" Juicy laughed.

"A freak huh?" inquired Argentina. "You ever done a girl?" "Done more than that…" said Juicy laughing, taking off her clothes and at the same time staring at the art on the walls, the fine furniture and the liquor cabinet filled with booze.

"I can see you living pretty good up in here," said Juicy, "with your sexy self."

"I do a'ight," said Argentina.

"You got jewelry too?" she asks, "anything with diamonds?"

Argentina is so wasted she thinks it's funny and is not threatened by the fact that Juicy is scoping out the place to rob her blind.

"Diamonds…sapphires…rubies," said Argentina laughing, taking Juicy by the hand and leading her into the bedroom.

When they get in the bedroom, Juicy is more turned on by Argentina's jewelry box, sitting on the dresser wide open, than she is her perky titties that fall out of the bra when she removes it.

Argentina moves in and starts rubbing Juicy's ass. "Your booty," she said, "is so juicy…"

"You like that, boo….?" asks Juicy. "I like it a lot," said Argentina. "Can you handle it?" asked Juicy.

Before Argentina could say a word, Juicy threw her on her back and pinned her against the mattress, diving right on top of her. She pulled Argentina's legs apart and began to finger her— with Argentina's head banging against the headboard.

"Hold up…" said Argentina. "I got something for you."

Juicy backs off a beat as Argentina dives for the top drawer and pulls out a long, black, dildo. As Argentina went one way, Juicy bent the other way towards the jewelry box and grabbed whatever she could and dumped it in her purse, which she had laying on the floor beside the bed.

"Welcome to the party, Bitch!" she screamed, snatching the dildo and fastening it on. She turned Argentina around and turned her Argentinean-ass out banging her hard as hell from the back. Argentina was hit with a double orgasm and came so hard she squirted all over the bed.

"Let me lick it up...let me lick it up!" screamed Juicy, pushing Argentina out of the way to lick it up like a lap dog.

Argentina laid out, almost passed out on the bed as Juicy was down on all fours licking it up. Argentina pulled herself together to start fingering Juicy from the back and started eating her out while Juicy hollered.

"You my kind of Bitch!" screamed Juicy.

Where you been all my life, Bitch?

All of my mother fucking life?

And with that they traded dildos and Argentina put on the dick and started hitting Juicy from the back. They were like two raw savages going at it like primitive beasts. It seemed to go on for hours, could have been days or just till the liquor wore off... and when it did—Holy Mother of God—Mia came back to the devastation. She opened her eyes in Argentina's bed as the two lay wrapped up, contorted around each other. They were bent like pretzels—legs, arms, breasts and pussies smashed up against the other.

Mia screamed.

She jumped up out of the bed, naked and shaking.

Her eyes caught sight of the "used" dildo and she almost fell out.

"Juicy," said Argentina. "What's wrong?"

"Oh my God...oh my god...." said Mia, gathering up her clothes just as quickly as she could, dressing herself in a panic.

"You want a drink?" asked Argentina.

"No! I don't want a drink!" screamed Mia. "I gotta get out of here." And with that Mia ran towards the door like she was running for Olympian gold...leaving Argentina sitting up naked on her knees. "See you tomorrow?" asked Argentina. No comment—just a slammed door.

chapter

14

HE NEXT DAY I DIDN'T have the strength to get out of bed. I was horrified by what I had done.

"Oh my God," I mumbled beneath my morning breath, "I slept with a woman."

What would my family say about this?

I'm going straight to hell.

I asked God for forgiveness but I still didn't feel any relief. Maybe God was really mad at me, because when I looked in my purse I couldn't help but noticed that I had a beautiful diamond necklace that spelled out the name Argentina.

I'm going to hell for sure. If I'm not going to hell I'm going to jail. I could tell this necklace was worth a lot of money. It was another thing that I couldn't give back but I could donate it to the raggedy shoebox college fund.

Oh God.

What had I gotten myself into?

I didn't want to face anyone.

I didn't even want to face myself.

All I could do was talk to God so I sat up and let the tears fall from my eyes. I couldn't understand why my life was so out of control. I had tried to get help from the preacher man, from the AA group and even from a Lesbian—but nothing had worked. I was in deeper than I had ever been in before.

I can't let go of the booze because even when I'm not holding it— it's holding me.

I'm addicted and no different than the crack head next door or around the corner.

I needed a way out but didn't see one. But there's got to be a way out.

I can't live this way, I said to myself as I reached for a bottle of pills that my sister kept on the nightstand beside the bed. Not knowing what they were, I thought I'd take my chances. I emptied the bottle into the palm of my hand and just stared at them.

I struggled with two things. If I killed myself wasn't that a one-way ticket to hell? After all, I deserved to go to Heaven. Now, Juicy on the other hand…she deserved to go straight to hell. And the second thing I struggled with was leaving Janiah to be raised by wolves *(a/k/a Ida Mae)* but I knew that she'd be okay. On the flip side, it would be the best thing for Janiah. She would never have to know what kind of demons lived inside of me. I never wanted her to see my problems— I hid them but as we know, everything in the dark eventually comes to the light.

So it would be better this way. Without any more thought, I swallowed all of the white pills in my hand and slowly drifted to sleep.

Lights out!

It was over. Good night, Mia.

Goodbye, Juicy.

chapter

15

O MY SHOCK AND DISAPPOINTMENT, four hours later I woke up. I thought to myself "heaven is so beautiful."

Dang…it looks just like my bedroom. Do they have a Sear's in heaven cause these are the same sheets I died on this morning?

Wait!

They have 100% cotton in heaven, too?

Wait a minute…now I know they don't have raggedy curtains in heaven, I said as I looked across the room and was greeted by the torn curtains that always greeted me in this room.

What the hell? I thought to myself. I can't even kill myself right.

But I did manage to make myself as sick as a dog.

Oh God.

I felt so nauseous. I picked up the empty pill bottle off the floor and read the label that I must have missed the first time around. In big black letters bold as day the bottle read, EXCEDRIN.

What the hell?

I wanted to sink down inside of myself, but I wouldn't have a chance because Janiah was knocking at the door.

"Come in," I said.

She entered slowly, looking at me with curious eyes. Janiah had looked at me this way before but I always tried to play it off— you know what I mean?

Bad case of the stomach flu. PMS.

Menstrual cramps.

I couldn't just say, "oh yeah...by the way...I have a talking booty that's fucking and robbing the city blind." And certainly a confession of being a straight-up, corrupt alcoholic was out of the question.

"What's wrong mommy?" Janiah asked as she sat on the bed. "Nothing baby," I said, "Just got cramps today."

"You get cramps a lot, huh mommy?"

"Let me ask you something, baby?" I said observing her Coca Cola shaped body, which was looking more and more like mine each day. She was the epitome of "round lips, mocha hips."

"What did you want to ask me?" she inquired.

"This might sound a little crazy," I said trying to preface it, "but have you ever heard voices?"

"Voices?" she asked with a confused look on her face. "Yeah," I said.

"The only voices I hear is Ida Mae cussing and fussing," she said with a laugh.

"No, I'm being serious, Janiah. Do you ever hear strange voices? Like someone is talking to you behind your back?"

"What?" she asked, looking at me cock-eyed at this point. "Now I know it sounds crazy, but...you know..."

"No mommy I don't know..." she said, "are you okay today?" "I'm good baby," I assured her, "have you ever tasted liquor before?"

"Not since I was five and grandma gave me that cognac." "What?" I screamed.

"I'm just playing," she said. "I don't drink and I don't hear voices, either!"

"You ever feel like having sex?" I asked trying to approach it from the other end.

"What????" she squealed embarrassed, "I don't plan on doing that for a long time."

"Well," I said, "you're almost 16...it's normal...I just want you to feel like you can talk to me about anything."

"I know that Mama..." she said, "are you talking to me about what Grandma's always saying?" "What does grandma say?" I asked.

"She always say how blessed I am…" said Janiah, "and that she hopes that I don't be like you."

"What does that mean?" I questioned.

"Well…" said Janiah, "Grandma's always saying a girl's gotta do what a girl's gotta do."

"No more unsupervised visits with grandma!" I quickly responded.

"Mama…you hear voices?" she asked.

I wanted to tell her the truth so bad but I just couldn't. *How could she possibly understand when I don't even understand it myself?* So I simply responded with a quick, "No baby…"

"Don't worry…I don't plan on doing anything crazy, Mama," said Janiah, "you know I got my mind set on being a lawyer."

"I know and I'm so proud of you," I said.

"You know," she said getting up off the bed, "I see how grandma talks to you and I hear the things that people say about you…and what they expect from you…"

"You do?" I asked surprised.

"Yeah," she said, "but I figured it out a long time ago…I'm going to use my brain and not my body."

❧

After Janiah left the room, I sat back and took a deep sigh. I was relieved that I didn't die in my sleep and that I had lived to have that conversation with my daughter. It was safe to say that Juicy didn't live in Janiah. Although, I couldn't be certain because she didn't drink. All I could do was pray that she never take a drink.

I was happy for Janiah but sad for me. I did drink and Juicy was alive and well. I could not promise how long I would go without taking a drink. So, I knew that Juicy would come back around again, I just didn't know when.

God, I said getting on my knees in prayer. *Please help me fight this demon that lives inside of me. You kept me here for a reason so send me an angel who can help me through this.*

I have no friends. No family.

No man.

And ultimately, no one to confide in. Just then my phone rang

God was in the business of answering prayers quickly. "Hello," I said.

"Mia!" blurted a familiar voice from the past. The voice was warm and friendly, but I couldn't place it right away.

"Hello?" I said again. "Mia…it's Trillion."

"Trillion!" I shouted.

"Where have you been?" she asked. "Me and my girlfriend Chance are always talking about you."

"Really?" I asked, "how is Chance?"

"Chance is still the same girl…. crazy as ever."

Uh oh, I thought. Still the same?

That's kind of scary.

"How you been?" she asked me again.

"Girl…it's a long story…I saw your sister at the grocery store yesterday and she gave me your number. Last I heard about you… you had a baby and had moved to Chicago."

"My baby is now a teenager," I said laughing. "You got any kids?"

"No girl," she said, "still trying to take care of myself."

"Dang Trillion," said Mia reminiscing, "I really miss you. I haven't had a friend like you since high school. I would love to get together for dinner and talk."

"Meet me for happy hour tonight," she said.

Uh oh, I thought. *I couldn't get too happy at happy hour.*

"Sure," I said with a bit of hesitancy. "You good?" she asked.

"Yeah…" I said, "meet me at the Red Onion on Wilshire."

It was an interesting meeting of sorts. I was shocked to see that almost fifteen years had passed and Trillion looked untouched by time. She was still beautiful. And she was as equally surprised to see that I still looked so young, my body was still intact and my booty was still the center of attention.

"Girl you still carrying that booty," she said hugging me, "that booty is like a wagon you dragging. Is it heavy, girl?"

I laughed.

I had such fond of memories of Trillion. She was so crazy and it was nice seeing her again. As I sat across from her, I had to admire her independence. She didn't care what people thought about her. She seemed somehow a little bit more free than me. Secretly, sometimes I wished I was her. Maybe not her, just a little more free.

It didn't take too long for Trillion to recognize that I hadn't touched a drop of alcohol, and by now she was on her third drink.

"Why aren't you drinking?" she asked. I paused.

"I have a problem," I said.

"What kind of problem?" she inquired.

"Something happens when I drink," I tried to explain. "Something happens to everybody when they drink," she said with a laugh.

"I'm serious Trillion," I said, "it's real deep." "Well tell it…" she said.

"Can I trust you to keep a secret?" I asked scooting in. "You have to ask…" she said slightly offended.

"All right girl," I said, "you were sent to me for a reason." "What's going on Mia?"

"It's like this…" I started, "It all started at your birthday party when I was 15 years old."

"What?"

"Yeah," I said, "you actually started it…. you gave me some spiked punch, remember?"

"I can't remember yesterday good…" was all she said.

"When you gave me that punch I started hearing voices." "Voices?"

"Real voices…" I said, "and it never stopped." "What are you talking about, Mia?"

"I'm trying to tell you that every time I drink, or get high… something happens. That night at your birthday party my booty started talking to me!" I blurted.

The man who was sitting next to us looked…all he heard was "talking booty" and it grabbed all of his attention. Trillion laughed and just looked at me like I was crazy, "please don't tell no one that story...I know your booty is big but God Damn...it talks too!"

I said, "Not only does it talk but it takes over and it has its own name."

"What's the booty's name?" she asked. "Juicy," I said.

Trillion falls out, and almost slides out of her chair and onto the floor. In fact, the man sitting next to us starts laughing too. She grabs her purse and looks at me with this ridiculous grin on her face, "Juicy...come on...let's go get something to eat."

I was devastated.

She didn't take me seriously at all.

"The booty is Juicy and all," she said jokingly, "but...girl... talking booty. You are too much! You on medication?"

"Forget about it Trillion," I said deflated. "I was just playing." "You had me going girl," she said as she got up and led the way out of the front door. "You don't have to make up excuses to get out of drinking with me. I don't mind drinking alone," said Trillion. As we left the Red Onion, I knew that the only way Trillion would believe it was to see it for herself.

chapter

16

*T*HE NEXT NIGHT I CALLED TRILLION and invited her out to the club. As I drove to Trillion's house to pick her up, I promised that this night I would be the one who would be in control. I would let Juicy out, but only under the supervision of Trillion. I trusted her like that. After all, she did have my best interest at heart.

"Hey girl," she said slipping inside the car.

"Hey girl. So you ready to party or what?" Trillion asked. "I'm ready to party all right," she said with a grin.

"Oh girl," said Trillion throwing up her hand, "you ain't gonna do nothing with your shy ass."

Boy, I thought to myself, *wait until she meets Juicy.*

"Girl…" said Trillion, "what's your booty talking about tonight?"

"Nothing girl," I said shaking my head knowing that she was making fun of me.

"Girl…how's your crazy mama?" asked Trillion.

"The same…she's still trying to auction me off every chance she gets."

"That's a damn shame," said Trillion, "you're mama's been trying to sell that ass since you were a teenager."

"Who you telling?" said Mia.

Ain't nothing wrong with a little booty, Trillion thought to herself. *I sure wish I had one.*

❧

When they pulled up the party was already underway. The music was banging, echoing out of the club and bouncing off all the cars in the jam-packed parking lot. People were hanging outside the door, inside the joint and everywhere else bodies could fit.

I felt a little nervous and began to have second doubts about letting Juicy out tonight. I wanted to show Trillion that I wasn't crazy, but maybe I was crazy to let her out in this kind of environment. When we entered the club the music was so loud I could hardly hear Trillion asking me what I wanted to drink.

"Ginger ale?" asked Trillion.

"No," I said, "Vodka and cranberry juice." "Ooooh," said Trillion, "big girl."

"You got to promise me something," I said to Trillion, "you'll protect me tonight."

"Protect you from what?" she asked, confused. "From myself," I whispered.

"What are you talking about?" she asked.

"You'll see soon enough," I said, "just have my back."

When the first drink came, I nearly inhaled it. It disappeared out of my glass like it had been vaporized.

"What the hell?" asked Trillion, "I thought you didn't drink." "That was yesterday," I said laughing. "Today I drink."

I probably wanted this drink more than Juicy did. "Another," I motioned to the bartender.

I quickly downed the second drink, too. Within moments, my head began to pound. It was starting…*uh oh*…I felt her coming and me leaving.

"What's up, hooker?" Juicy said to Trillion. "You're that bitch, Trillion. I like that name…I guess that pussy's worth more than a million." Trillion's eyes widened. In her observation, it appeared Mia had dropped all inhibitions. She was sitting at the bar stool, wearing a tight skirt with her legs gapped open.

"Mia?" Trillion asked. "Girl… Ease up on that Vodka."

"I'm not Mia, Bitch," she said staring at me with harsh, black eyes. "I ain't seen your ass since my coming out party."

"Are you okay, girl?"

"Never better, now that the bitch is away!" she said turning to the bartender and motioning for another drink.

Trillion was tripping.

She was just staring at Mia/Juicy with eyes wide open, confused.

"I'm Juicy, Bitch," she said, extending a hand to Trillion who was in shock.

"Oh my God," Trillion mumbled beneath her breath.

She's got two personalities, Trillion thought to herself. "You got a cig-arette, Bitch?" asked Juicy.

Trillion shook her head.

"You are a fine mother fucker!" said Juicy checking out Trillion from all angles.

Trillion was speechless.

"What's up?" asked Juicy, "you never seen a talking booty before?"

Trillion almost fell off the barstool.

"Wait…wait…" said Trillion staring at her drink, "what's in this drink?"

Juicy laughed.

"You're a stupid acting, Bitch," said Juicy.

"Listen, I ain't gonna be too many more Bitches…" said Trillion in a huff, "I don't know if I like this side of you, Mia."

"Bitch…you call me Mia one more good time…" said Juicy, "you definitely ain't gonna like this side of me."

Juicy took another drink and Trillion exited into the crowd in a huff.

"That's a stuck up Bitch if I ever seen one," said Juicy, "flat ass ho!"

Juicy stood up and started dancing at the bar stool, eyeing the crowd—searching through the misty, smoke-filled room for the big wallets and big dicks. The room was jam packed with people pressed against the walls. She spotted a tall, handsome black man with a muscular build, diamonds flowing and two bulges— fat wallet and fat dick. She made eye contact with him. Within seconds, he inched his way to where she was standing.

"What do you want, big daddy?" asked Juicy.

"You called me over here," he said checking out the booty. "My booty called you over here. Personally...I don't give a fuck about you."

He laughed.

Juicy grabbed the tall black man by the hand and began to lead him through the thick crowd of people where she took him to a private booth in the back. She pushed him inside and he quickly surrendered. Seconds later, Juicy unzipped his pants.

"Whoa," he said startled, "you don't waste any time."

"I know what I want," said Juicy. "Some money and some dick...in that order."

He laughed.

Juicy pulled out his big dick and dropped to her knees. As she was pulling and sucking, she was also searching and rummaging through his pants, and taking everything that she *felt* was of value—from dollar bills to credit cards. The guy didn't know the difference. He was pressed against the wall with his eyes rolled in the back of his head as Juicy's mouth opened like something out of a National Geographic special and she swallowed all ten inches whole.

Holy Mother of God!

He was about to come and come hard.

In the meantime, Trillion had taken it upon herself to go and check on her friend just to make sure she was done tripping. She searched high and low for Mia but there was no sign of her and just as she was about to give up and catch a cab home, she spotted Mia through the misty smoke in the thick, darkness of the room on her knees with dick all down her throat. Trillion almost passed out!

"Oh my God," she said. "That cannot be Mia!"

Her initial thought—maybe he was raping Mia, but after a second glance it looked more like Mia was raping him.

"Holy shit," she said.

"Mia! Mia!" she screamed, running to the booth and snatching Juicy off her knees.

"I told you my name ain't Mia, Bitch!" screamed Juicy as she wiped her mouth, "I'm taking care of some business right now, Bitch! Get the fuck out of here!"

The guy was as horrified as Trillion. He got soft immediately, zipped up his pants and got the hell out—limp dick and all.

Trillion grabbed Juicy and started shaking her.

"What's wrong with you?" screamed Trillion, "you're acting crazy!"

All the shaking began to make Juicy disoriented. Her eyes rolled into the back of her head and once she opened them again, Mia had returned. The harsh, black eyes had mellowed to a soft brown and the attitude was gone. The sex, wild, nymphomaniac tamed and was replaced by the shy, sad persona of a woman filled with shame.

"You believe me now?" asked Mia.

❧

The drive home was dead silence. It was uncomfortable and I found myself waiting for a response from Trillion.

"Mia this is serious… does your family know about this?" "No one knows but Juicy and I."

"Girl, you need help," said Trillion.

"I've tried everything from rehab to God," I confessed. "I even tried to kill myself right before you called…. but even that didn't even work."

Trillion reached out and grabbed my hand offering much needed comfort.

"I wanted to turn the lights out," I continued, "but I can't do that, Trillion. I have to be here for Janiah… she needs me. She's about to start college."

"Wait," said Trillion, "this only happens when you drink, right?"

"Yes," I said quietly beneath my breath. "Then stop," Trillion insisted.

"I can't just stop," I confessed. "I'm addicted to the booze…and the booze is addicted to me."

"Get the hell out of here," said Trillion, "just stop drinking." "No," I said, "really I can't."

"I don't understand," said Trillion. "Why can't you just stop?" "The same reason you can't stop breathing," I said flatly.

"Well," said Trillion defensively, "I would *die* if I stopped breathing, obviously."

"Girl," said Trillion shaking her head, "you need some serious help. I had no idea that you were so messed up."

"I cried out to God for help and that's when the phone rang… and it was you."

Trillion's eyes cut to me sharply.

"God sent you to me, Trillion…" I said.

"No…No…No…" said Trillion shaking her head, "this is too deep for me. We need to call your mama."

"Hell naw!" I protested, "my mama would love Juicy…she would keep me liquored up and her and Juicy would be the best of friends."

"Why don't you tell your sisters?" she questioned.

"If my family knew they would take Janiah away from me and put me in the nearest nut house," I said.

"Girl, all I know is you're too old for this shit…going on 30 years old!"

"I'm only 28."

"Girl…the way you're throwing dicks in your mouth…you won't make it to 30."

I sank deep into the seat and sighed under the weight of it all. I was grateful that Trillion could actually witness what I was going through. Maybe I would get the support I needed after all.

"I'm your best friend," said Trillion, "you're not in this alone. We came back together for a reason." "Thanks Trillion," I said. "You will never have another drink as long as I have something to do with it," promised Trillion, "because I don't like that damn Juicy."

I laughed.

"She is a Bitch, right?" I confirmed. "You have NO idea!"

❧

That night when I returned home, my sisters NeNe and Ducky were chatting it up in the living room. I entered the room relieved and light of heart.

"NeNe…" I said, "thanks for hooking me and Trillion back up again."

"Who Trillion?" asked Ducky. "You back with that sneaky ho?"

"She's my best friend," I said.

NeNe and Ducky exchanged a quick glance and they both shook their head at the same time.

"What's wrong with Trillion?" I asked, "you haven't even seen her in 15 years."

"And neither have you…" declared NeNe, "for you to come up in here and start calling the Bitch your best friend. Don't have her ass up in here stealing my shit…"

"You guys don't know nothing…God sent Trillion back to me."

"God!" screamed Ducky, "what's God got to do with that back biting Bitch?"

"Why don't you like Trillion?"

"I used to date this guy that knew her back in the day," said Ducky, "and he used to call her the head doctor."

"The head doctor?" I asked. "She wasn't trying to be no doctor."

NeNe and Ducky started laughing.

"She was sucking all the dicks in the neighborhood, fool!" said NeNe.

"Ya'll just jealous of her because she was so pretty…"

"She was the prettiest head doctor in the neighborhood," confirmed Ducky.

"I ain't thinking about ya'll… Mama's got this guy that's getting ready to rent me an apartment. I'm about to get my own place so I can have my own friends."

NeNe and Ducky just shook their heads again.

"She's so naïve," I heard NeNe tell Ducky when I left the room.

"She'll find out the hard way," said Ducky.

Whatever, I thought. *It was time for me to move on with my life.*

chapter

17

$\mathcal{T}$HE NEXT MORNING IDA MAE called me bright and early to meet the man for the new apartment. But it took me so long to get ready and out of the house, by the time I picked her up we were running late for the meeting.

"Girl," said Ida Mae, "I got an apartment and a man for your broke ass…and you taking your sweet ass time."

By the time we arrived the guy was looking upset sitting in his white Range Rover. When Ida saw he was sitting in a Range Rover, she started grinning ear to ear.

"Jackpot," she mumbled beneath her breath.

"Mama please…" I said, "I'm trying to get this place…."

"You stupid mother fucker…you oughta be trying to get more than this apartment. You should be trying to get this whole damn building!"

"Ida Mae!"

"This man owns this building and a whole lot of others," said Ida Mae as she held out her hand, waving to the guy.

"Come on you dumb Bitch," she said checking me out head to toe, "and why didn't you wear some tighter pants? Shit! We're trying to get your dumb-ass a discount."

I quickly jumped out of the car and tried to get away from Ida as I walked up to the Range Rover, where this fine, chocolate man brother who looked something like Denzel, opened the door and got out.

Damn!

He was some kind-of-fine wearing a tailored charcoal-colored suit with some snakeskin boots.

Good God almighty!

And when he smiled, I melted right there on the mother loving sidewalk.

"Hi," he said extending a hand, "my name is Luke."

I could barely speak, but it didn't matter because that's when Ida Mae jumped in front of me and spoke for me and every other woman on the block.

"Hi you doing? I'm Ida Mae…and this is Mia," said Ida, snatching the hand that was meant for me to shake. "We apologize for being late. We know you're a very important man with a lot of business to take care of."

"Oh that's all right," he said grinning ear to ear. "It's my pleasure to be in the company of such beautiful women."

"So, you two are sisters?" he asked.

"Now you know my old ass ain't her sister," said Ida Mae changing her tune. "This is my daughter that I was telling you about on the phone."

"Oh yes…you're renting the place…" he said, "you didn't tell me how fine your daughter was…"

"Thank you," I said a little embarrassed, but thrilled that he liked me.

As we walked towards the apartment, I was pleased to see that the "Golden Brook Apartments" sat on well-kept grounds and a manicured lawn. The vacant unit was in the courtyard and there were beautiful purple and gold flowers growing just outside my door. It felt like home already.

When he opened the door, I was equally delighted to find a very clean home with new floors, new carpet, new blinds and appliances. There were two bedrooms, which was great because Janiah could finally have her own room. I nodded my head, as I looked around, realizing that this could be the beginning of the new me.

"How much is the rent?" I asked.

"$1,500 a month," he said without hesitation. "What's the cute customer discount?" Ida Mae jumped in to ask.

He paused, checking me out while "pretending" to be cooler than he actually was. I could tell that he was feeling me as much as I was feeling him.

"If she really likes it…we can work something out," he didn't hesitate to say.

"Well she really likes it…" declared Ida boldly.

"Well let's work something out," he said to me, as he escorted us out the door with a final word, "Mia…meet me at my place of business tomorrow at 3 o'clock and we can go over the terms of the contract."

He handed me his business card, and I smiled.

"Jackpot," whispered Ida Mae as she caught his eyes staring at my booty when we walked away. Ida gave me one hard look and of course, another piece of bad advice, "don't fuck this up, Bitch…a woman's gotta do what a woman's gotta do."

❧

The next day I pulled out my tight-fitting sweater dress, which fit every curve that I owned, in order to swing the popular vote in my direction.

Reduced rent.

Reduced rent.

Reduced rent.

I pulled out the business card again and smiled when I read the big gold letters that boldly declared—*Luke Johnson, President, TriGold Realty Corporation.*

I sure do love a business man.

I wonder what his office looked like. It was probably in the heart of a ritzy-looking block with a grand entrance, valet parking and security guards in suits. I couldn't wait to see his fine butt again.

I jumped in the car and gassed it up and headed on my way. The address was a Los Angeles address, but I wasn't familiar with the area and was somewhat surprised when my mapped directions took me down a street with all of these industrial buildings and warehouses.

What?

I looked at the address again—this time twice because the address on the card delivered my car right in front of *Strippers in Gold.*

What the hell?

Strippers in Gold?

What happened to TriGold Realty?

This has got to be the wrong address on his business card, but I couldn't buy that because directly in front of the building sat the white Range Rover I saw yesterday.

"Okay…what in the hell has my mama done this time?" I asked out loud, "I'm damn sure not *stripping* to get an apartment."

I was so mad I didn't even want to get out of the car, and I probably wouldn't have if Luke hadn't come out the front door with a Latin woman wearing stripper shoes, damn near naked and boobs the size of all of downtown.

"You've got to be kidding," I said, mumbling beneath my breath as Luke locked eyes with me and waved at me to get out of the car and come in.

Oh shit.

I got out of the car and walked cautiously to the front door. He greeted me with a big smile and warm embrace, but honestly, he just lost all points with me having me meet him at a strip club of all places to negotiate an apartment lease.

"TriGold Realty?" I questioned, holding up the card very close to his eyes.

"Don't worry about all that," he said, "it's in the back."

I raised one eye and looked at him like he was stone crazy.

Once inside, it was so dark it was hard to follow him…all I could do was follow his shadow. The music was loud and thumping, and there were all kinds of women walking around half-naked, with some on the strip pole.

What a scene, I thought to myself.

I could feel all eyes on me as I walked past a group of strippers who were looking at me like I was next girl in line to ride the pole. One of the strippers pulled my arm. When I looked up at her, all I saw was a Cuban woman with light skin, long hair and big tits. She was wearing black lingerie with a big hole in the middle revealing a bare vagina. There were two more big holes in the back of her "suit" revealing each naked booty cheek.

Nice outfit, I want to say.

"Your first day?" she asked.

"My last," I said sarcastically and kept it moving.

By the time we reached Luke's office, I had big attitude. I was really put out by this poor attempt to get me on his pole.

"I'm here to lease an apartment...not give you a lap dance," I said with a fierceness in my voice.

Luke looked at me and laughed. He shook his head, took a seat real cool-like and invited me to sit down, but I preferred standing so I didn't budge.

"Have a seat, young lady," he said, "I'm a businessman first..." Slowly, I surrendered and sat down, sliding my application across his desk where he scrutinized it closely while I continued to check my immediate surroundings in search of a real estate office. At least, I was able to spot a small business license on the wall, squeezed in between many other licenses including TriGold Realty, Goldie's Check Cashing, and Gold Construction.

What the hell? I thought. Did he strike gold or what? "How's your credit?" he asked, interrupting my thought. "Decent," I said.

"Income?"

"Decent," I responded.

"How many occupants will be signing the lease?"

"Just me..." I said, "but I do have a teenage daughter who will be living with me."

He didn't budge and his face remained firm as he kept his focus on the business at hand. I almost felt uncomfortable and wanted to "lighten" it up a bit.

"I'll set the security deposit at $1,000," he said, "and the apartment is $1,500 a month…due on the first of each month…6% late fee… one year lease."

I was shocked.

He was a businessman and though he appeared partial to Juicy in the beginning—that did not seem to affect his ability to charge me out the ass.

"What happened to the cute customer discount?" I asked jokingly.

"I got the rent, no problem…but that security deposit is eating me up."

He showed no compassion. I was surprised that my knitted sweater dress wasn't breaking him down, but it was obvious he was immune— because he had a million Juicy's walking around with ho's in the front and ho's in the back.

"Don't judge a strip joint by its cover," was all he could say when he looked into my begging eyes.

Oh.

I felt that one.

Guess I messed up by being judgmental.

"It's just very strange that I had to walk past pole dancers to rent this apartment," I couldn't help but say.

"This is my empire," he said, "I run all of my businesses out of this office. But don't let the smooth taste fool you…it's a 100% legit."

❧

The drive back home was both exciting and nerve-wrecking. I got the place, but it was going to be a stretch to come up with the deposit and the rent to move in by the 1st of the month, which was just two days away. I would have to ask my brothers for an advance from the family business so I could swing that deposit.

For a second, I thought about the raggedy shoe box in the closet. I never touched that money and I never would. That was my sacred stash—Janiah's college fund. It was the only way I could justify keeping the money and turning "bad" money into "good" money. I was so deep in thought that I almost missed the call, but I'm glad I didn't because it was Luke.

"Hey," I said, "what's up?"

"Ready to give you these keys," he said. "Okay," I said quickly, "where can I meet you?" "Crustaceans in Beverly Hills...4 o'clock."

"Great..." I said, "I know it well...my mother's favorite restaurant."

I hung up and knew I had to make quick moves to get the money, but when I called my brothers they were both tied up for a few hours. The best I could do was meet up with Luke, give him the rent and let him know I'd get him the deposit later in the week.

It sounded like a good plan to me. So, I drove home and freshened up a bit and met Luke at 4 o'clock. I couldn't wait to get there because they have the best crabs in town and the atmosphere is like no other. It's beautiful and walking into the restaurant is like walking on top of an aquarium with amazing fish swimming around on the floor.

When I entered the restaurant all eyes were on me. I had changed into Ida Mae's favorite pair of tight fitting jeans, since the business-look didn't work to get my "cute" tenant discount maybe the jeans would work and I'd get a free meal. *I hate using Juicy,* I said to myself feeling rather conflicted, *but a woman's gotta do what a woman's gotta do.*

I found Luke sitting at the bar with his friend, who Luke quickly introduced as "James."

"Hi," said James with his tongue hanging out like a dog in heat.

"Mia," I said shaking his sweaty palms, trying to pull back my hand.

"Cool off man," said Luke observing oozing sex vibe, "this is my new tenant."

"I think I know you," said James staring intently at me. My heart jumped.

Leaped.

Then stopped.

Oh shit, I said to myself. *He doesn't know me but he might know Juicy.*

Suddenly, my mouth got dry and I broke into a light sweat, especially on my forehead.

"You okay?" asked Luke.

"Fine," I said, quickly recovering and turning away from James.

"No…I know you…" he said pointing and making what I would call a "mother loving" scene. Obviously, I was sensitive.

My eyes widened but my throat tightened.

"Where…where….where…" I stumbled around my words. "That's it!" he said snapping his fingers.

Oh shit!

"Yeah…yeah…" he said dragging it out. Luke was waiting patiently with keen interest on where his friend knew me.

"Donald Trump's real estate seminar," he blurted. Luke smiled with relief.

I smiled with major relief. And goofy James smiled too.

"Here are your keys and your signed lease," he said sliding it across the bar.

"Thank you!" I said with lit up eyes.

"All I need is your rent and for you to keep being 'cute' because I waived the security deposit."

I smiled.

"Thank you so much, Luke."

He nodded, and I could tell he didn't want a whole lot of hoopla or fanfare around the discount. He was "quiet" with his generosity and that was very attractive to me.

chapter

18

$\mathcal{I}$ WAS SO EXCITED ABOUT moving into my own place that I could barely wait to get home and tell Janiah to start packing! When I got home, Janiah was sitting on the couch eating ice cream and reading a book.

"Guess what!" I said with great enthusiasm, "we're moving!"
"What!"

"We got a new place," I said waving the keys in the air, "and you got your own room."

"Are you serious?" she asked so excited.

"Things are going to be different, baby…" I said. "They're going to be better."

"My own room?"

"Get to packing…we're getting up out of here!" I said with a smile.

Just then, there was a knock on the door and when I opened it, Trillion was on the other side. I was glad NeNe wasn't home, because she's not a fan of Trillion and I didn't feel like hearing her mouth.

"Whatcha doing girl?" asked Trillion barging right on in. "Moving," I said, "got my place."

"Oh wow…" she said, "I'm happy for you."

"Things are looking up," I said dancing around the bedroom. Trillion gave me a hard look, then quickly closed the door to speak with me in private.

"So…" she said getting ready to start some stuff, "you talked to Juicy lately?"

"No…" I said, "I'm going to beat this demon."

"When was the last time you had a drink?" she asked. "Since the last time I was with you."

"Good," she said.

"I'm serious this time, Trillion," I said, "I got too much going on. I'm about to get my real estate license...my kid's going to college, got my own place and a fine Landlord with his own personal goldmine."

"I'm happy for you sister, but I still think you should see someone and get help."

"I'm good," I said, "I'm finally finding peace."

"Okay girl," said Trillion looking around the room, "let me help you pack your shit."

"That's a great idea," I said, "and if you don't mind helping me bring some of these boxes over to the new place."

"That's cool" she said, "I'd love to check out your new spot."

❧

I moved the following week and it was one of the most joyful days of my life. I'm going to miss NeNe. She was a great sister/ roommate who, for the most part, stayed out of my business.

I just loved my new place. It was warm, charming and all things nice, and with the exception of a broken kitchen light it was just perfect for us. Janiah was so excited about having her own room that I barely saw her anymore and when I did see her these days, I couldn't help but notice her body going through a major transformation. At the end of the day, her body had a haunting resemblance to mine.

One morning as Janiah prepared for school, I actually saw exactly what my Aunt Mary saw in me when I was growing up. But this time, I finally understood why she was so concerned when I was a child. Janiah was wearing a tight pair of jeans with a short shirt that didn't cover her booty, which jiggled as she walked away from the breakfast table.

Uh oh, I thought.

Snap it up.

Suck it in.

Squeeze it down.

Girdle time.

But I didn't want to give her a complex like the one I had when Aunt Mary drug me to the mall, forcing me to squeeze myself into an old lady booty cast.

No way, I thought. Don't start nothing and it won't be nothing. Why bring attention to her booty and create all the hang-ups that come along with it? I refused to be a part of the booty conspiracy—helping to create an entire "personality" around Janiah's rear end.

🥀

As soon as Janiah left there was a knock at the door. In fact, I thought that maybe she had forgot something and had turned right around and come back. So, imagine my surprise when I opened the door and there stood my fine, chocolate landlord wearing a t-shirt, some velour sweat pants and a hat.

*Uuummmm….*I thought to myself.

"Luke," I said, sounding surprised.

He held up a light fixture and offered a smile. "I know it's early but I wanted to come and make sure your kitchen light was working…"

"Sure," I said with a shy smile, as I opened the door and let him in.

As we walked towards the kitchen, I got a whiff of his good smelling cologne.

Good God it almost knocked me down!

Mmmmmmmm….

I could work with this.

I offered him a step stool and the brother went to work. I couldn't help but notice the way that the muscles bulged from his biceps and triceps as he replaced the old light fixture with the new. His dark chocolate skin rippled with every bend and turn and I was mesmerized, as I took it all in standing on the ground looking up.

I better back up off this man, I thought, *or he'll be trying to have me on one of his poles.*

"So…." I said trying to make small talk, "I'm surprised you're up so early…"

"And why is that?"

"Well… a man like you probably keep pretty late nights…"

"In the bed every night by ten and up at four for my morning jog."

"You go to bed at 10 o'clock every night?" I asked with my nose turned up in disbelief.

"You don't believe me?" he asked.

"Nope," I said crossing my arms.

"Why?" he asked, "cause I own a strip club?" "Maybe," I said.

"I own it," he said, "I'm not dancing in it."

"So who's taking care of your business while your sleep?" "That's what managers are for," he said checking me out. "I get the feeling you think you know a lot about me…" "Maybe I do," I said with a little attitude.

"You shouldn't judge me…" Luke said, "I hate people to look at my glory and don't know my story…or look at my story and don't know my glory."

"So what's your story?"

"My mother was a Pentecostal minister," he offered. "Get out…" I said, "you're a preacher's kid?"

"Born and raised in the church," he said, "but what I could never understand when I was growing up was how religious people can be the most judgmental people in the world."

"That's so true."

"My mother was very compassionate with church folks…but not me. I got turned off and traded religion for spirituality."

"That makes sense to me," I said, "but it's hard for me to see you in a *spiritual* light."

"That's because you're looking at me with clouded vision…" he said without skipping a beat, "you're looking at me through the eyes of religion."

I guess he was right but I wasn't ready to bend on my views just yet.

"When my mother died," he continued, "she had a lot of property and a big insurance policy…her death opened the door to me getting into the real estate game…acquiring properties, selling properties and other businesses."

"Like strip clubs?" I asked raising one eye.

"It's a lucrative business," he said, "but it's deeper than that." "I bet it is," I said with biting sarcasm.

"I opened the club to help lost souls…" he defended. "To help lost souls or hustle lost souls?"

"Don't judge," was all he said before continuing. "I was married to a religious woman a long time ago…we had a beautiful baby girl… Golden was her name. One day, my *religious* wife up and left and took my six month old baby girl with her."

"What?"

"No forwarding address… no phone number… nothing." "Did you try to find your daughter?"

"Are you kidding me? Of course I did! I searched for years, but later I found out that my ex-wife had changed their identity after she left."

"Why did she leave?" I asked.

"I don't really have an answer for that…all she left was a note saying that she wasn't happy and she didn't love me anymore."

"I'm sorry," I said growing humbler by the minute. "What happened to your daughter?"

"Long and short it…nineteen years later I got an invitation to her funeral."

What?

I was horrified by the words. I couldn't even imagine as a parent the pain of losing a child.

"What happened?"

"She worked at a strip joint, and one night after dancing…she was murdered by one of the clients who just assumed she was a whore," was all that he said with tears in his eyes.

"Now I understand why you help lost souls," I mumbled almost embarrassed by my prejudice toward him.

There was a long pause of silence between both our next word and our next breath.

"How did you find out?" I asked him.

"My ex-wife's sister found me and gave me the news."

"Whatever happened to your ex-wife? Did you ever speak to her again?"

"She died five years before my daughter," he said quietly, "drug overdose."

Oh my God.

"I found out after my daughter's death that she wanted to be a doctor and was paying her way through college by stripping. She wasn't a whore."

It was in this moment that I realized I had grossly misjudged Luke. I was guilty of what people had done to me my whole life— *judged a booty by its cover and a book its cover.*

Same thing.

Luke and I were a lot alike.

In fact, we were more the same than different.

"I have to say Luke…I'm sorry but I really misjudged you. I did to you what the world does to me every day."

"What do you mean?" he inquired.

"When people look at me, they always assume I'm a stripper, a slut or that I get paid off my body somehow."

"I never saw you that way, Mia," he quickly inserted, "I saw your beauty first, not your booty."

I smiled.

It was the sweetest words any man had ever said to me.

"I think you're all set," he said flipping the light on, changing the subject entirely.

"Oh yeah," I said in daze, almost forgetting the real reason he had come over in the first place. It was just to change a light fixture but in the end he ended up turning on two lights—the kitchen light and my light.

It was an unmistakable glow that Luke caught sight of when he turned and looked at me. I must have been blushing and my cheeks were a bright, flushed crimson.

I was so turned on by his goodness.

It was obvious that he was much more than a savvy businessman. He was a gentle soul with a deep, rich past that was oozing out of his smooth chocolate skin and dripping all over my linoleum floor. I was shy by nature, but I could not deny that at this point I was dripping too. And he must have sensed that—as his light brown eyes began to scan the length of my body with intensity and intention. And for a moment, we stood eye to eye, and though he was much taller still we stood on even ground. There was something thick between us drawing on both of us. It was magnetizing him to draw closer to me and me to pull closer to him.

His lips began to part like a velvet curtain opening for a grand production.

Oh dear God.

What do I do now?

I couldn't help but glance at the clock…it was 9:31 a.m. in the morning.

Who gets this damn hot this early?

What the hell?

It was too early to call this a "lunchtime quickie"…couldn't we at least wait till noon?

No.

I couldn't.

I was melting inside.

I couldn't breathe anymore and when I got a second whiff of his Sunday best cologne that was all she wrote.

Our lips touched ever so gently as he opened his mouth wider and his lips laid over the top of mine and began to softly suckle my lips. His mouth opened and our tongues intertwined to taste one another. In this moment, my cell phone began to ring but I politely ignored it.

Do continue, I wanted to say.

I wanted to take my time to feel every ounce of saliva that we dared to share with each other. It was then that he let out a moan. It was like Tarzan calling to Jane in the wild and I surrendered all inhibitions as his strong black hands began to rub my back— stroking up and down my spine till he leaned me over the top of the kitchen table and began to suck my neck.

Oh my God.

Oh my God.

His hands circled the skin beneath my shirt and around my breasts. I could feel my nipples getting hard and hot. Within moments, he took my shirt off and placed his lips around my nipples.

Sucking.

Sucking.

Sucking.

"Oh Luke…" I moaned. "I want to feel you inside me."

The moment I said that the phone started ringing, but we both ignored it. His tongue started to make its way down to the bottom half, but first he passed across my stomach and kissed my navel.

Oh Luke.

But he didn't stop there. No…further he went. Oh Luke.

Oh Luke.

By this time my legs were gapped wide open as Luke continued his investigation of my intimate places. And by the time his tongue reached between my legs, I was gasping for breath, and half out of my mind I called his name again.

Oh Luke.

Luke.

Luke.

Luke.

"Stop!" I cried out interrupting the orgasm that was surely on its way. I sat up on the table and quickly unbuttoned his pants and took his penis and put it in my mouth.

His hips began to move and he started making sounds like me.

Mia.

Mia.

Mia.

For the next 45 minutes we would take turns calling out the other's name.

Oh Luke.

Mia baby.

Oh Luke.

Mia more.

Luke....right there.

Mia...don't stop.

When we could no longer take not being inside of one another, he laid on top of me on the table and slowly but deliberately, intensely, passionately, romantically and dramatically put everything he had deep inside of me.

Luuuuukkkkkk......

Miiiiiiiiiiiiaaaaaaaaaaaaaaaaaa....

Then we dissolved from two people into one. Right there on the table.

We became our own version of an art piece.

Beautifully sculpted as he moved to the rhythm of my beating heart and flowing ocean.

"You feel so good, baby..." he moaned in my ear as his body changed rhythm on the edge of an orgasm. He started to moan louder and louder.

"I'm cooommming, Mia...." "I'm commming too, baby..."

Our legs wrapped around each other's as we locked into place like two wild animals who never wanted to be set free. After the explosion, we locked eyes as he slowly kissed me.

As I lay my head on his chest, I couldn't believe I could make passionate love without Juicy's involvement. It was hard to imagine that someone could enjoy me without Juicy making a guest appearance. Luke proved to me that I was wrong. But before I could get too cozy, the doorbell rang.

"You expecting company?" he asked as we both jumped up and quickly re-dressed.

"No," I said somewhat surprised. "No one even knows where I live.

Maybe it's my mom…"

"I should be going anyways…" he said.

"You don't have to…" I said, making my way quickly to the front door where I opened it, only to find Trillion standing on my doorstep with a plant in her hand.

"Trillion!" I said, shocked to see her. "What are you doing here?"

"I tried calling but you didn't pick up…"

Just then, Luke stepped from around the corner. Trillion's eyes damn near popped out of her head when she saw that fine chocolate brother. She almost choked on the very words she tried to say…"Hello…"

Luke smiled, as he headed toward the door.

"I'm Trillion," she said extending a hand, *"Mia's* friend."

"Hey, I'm Luke…" he said politely as he kissed me on the cheek making his way out the door. And just like that he was gone. I waved and offered a smile, and Trillion did the same but I poked her in the side so that she could stick her tongue back in her mouth.

"What the fuck!" screamed Trillion. "Who was *that?*"

"My lips are sealed, heifer," I said teasing her.

"Now wait a minute…. is that one of your friends or one of Juicy's friends?"

He don't know no Juicy.

He don't want no Juicy.

He don't see no Juicy.

"He's digging Mia," I said proudly.

"So what's the story between Mia and Luke?" Trillion pressed.

"No story," I said, "that's my fine ass Landlord I told you about." "The goldmine?" she inquired, "oh…I know you got a discount on the rent this month," she said with a laugh. "Why do you say that?" I asked.

"I know you fucked him." "Correction…." I said, "he fucked me."

"Be careful girl…" cautioned Trillion. "You might not be ready for all of this. You sure you need to be dealing with a man right now?"

"What are you saying?" I asked defensively. "I'm good…I told you I wasn't drinking anymore."

"Yeah, but maybe you should focus on getting yourself together first…you still in therapy?" she questioned. "Every week," I said, "I told you I was getting better." "Just don't get ahead of yourself…" she warned.

"If I didn't know you better, Trillion…" I said, suggesting foul play.

"What?" Trillion pressed defensively.

"You don't seem too happy for me…" I offered.

"Don't be ridiculous, Mia…I'm just trying to look out for your best interests."

"I think my interests are just fine," I said.

The air was thick in the room. I was feeling a different "vibe" from Trillion, but I let it go.

"I'm good if you're good," she said handing me the plant. "Thank you," I said squashing the weird vibe between us. "Girl, I got the hottest tickets in town," she said sitting down on my couch. "The All Star Game in Atlanta…. this weekend!" "What!"

"I got plane tickets, airfare, hotel, rental car…everything!" she said waving the tickets wildly in the air.

"What?" I said, "You know I don't party like that…since I been in therapy and all."

"Oh come on, Mia…"

"No…. No…" I said shaking my head. "I don't get down like that no more."

"You have got to come… You don't have to take a single drink!"

"I can't…. I can't."

"I'll take care of you! I'll watch out for you!" Trillion promised, "Just don't make me go by myself…"

"I don't know…"

"You're the most beautiful friend I have…." said Trillion, "nobody's got a body like yours…you and I would clean up at the All Stars… maybe catch us a couple of ballers."

"We too old for that shit…"

"The cougars are taking over…" she said.

"This is cougar time!" I laughed.

"Girl, you want us to go out there and get those baby cubs?" I asked.

"Hell yeah! That's what I'm talking about!"

"Maybe," I reasoned, "if you're going to be with me and make sure I don't drink…"

"Girl…I got you."

"You know I ain't trying to see that damn Juicy again." Trillion nodded her head in agreement.

"Those days are behind me….literally," says Mia with a laugh as she turned to look at her booty.

Trillion laughed too.

"It's nice to see you being more like your old self again…" said Trillion, "reminds me of when we were kids."

"It's good to feel like my old self…" I added. "So this weekend, right?" Trillion confirms. I paused then slowly nodded my head. "Yeah…" I said.

"Well all right!" said Trillion slapping Mia on the booty.

"I'll pick you up Friday morning…flight leaves at 11 a.m." said Trillion.

"Okay," I said.

"Be ready," said Trillion walking out the door. "Thanks for the plant!" I called after her.

"Thank me by being ready on time…" she said as she walked away. "By the way girl, I hope you don't fall in love."

"What are you talking about, Trillion?"

"The last time you fell in love I never saw you again…took me 15 years to find you, remember?" she asked.

"That wasn't me falling in love," I protested "Juicy started that one…but this time I'm running the show," I said pushing Trillion out the door but not before she turned around and threw me a sucker punch.

"Oh…. you remember my girl, Chance?" she asked. "Uh huh," I replied cautiously.

"She's going to meet us in Atlanta," she said, dropping the news like a bomb out of mid-air.

Oh shit, I thought to myself. *The mouthpiece?* I couldn't help but re-member back when we were kids and Chance didn't give a damn about giving the whole neighborhood a *chance*.

"Hell naw!" I shouted, but Trillion didn't stop to listen. She just kept it moving.

🥀

Later that afternoon, I was tossing around Trillion's invitation in my head. If I were being honest with myself, I really didn't want to take on Atlanta this weekend with Trillion *and* Chance. I felt like I could travel with Trillion, but Chance coming with us introduced a whole new element to the weekend, and I wasn't comfortable with that vibe.

I've been sober for almost two months and haven't heard a word from Juicy.

I liked it like that.

I felt like I could trust my life with Trillion, but I damn sure didn't trust that Chance. I almost wanted to find a way out of it, and back straight out of this commitment. Maybe I could check in with Luke and see what he's up to this weekend. I'd rather spend the weekend in bed with Luke instead of partying with Trillion and Chance. But at the same time, Trillion would never let me live it down if I chose Luke over her.

"Mom," said Janiah, interrupting my chaotic thoughts. I hadn't even realized that she had already made it home from school.

"Hi baby...how was school?"

"Good mom..." she said staring at me, "you seem real happy today. What did you do today?"

I froze in my tracks.

"Uuuuuhhhh.... it was a real good today," I said blushing, as she made her way into the kitchen to fix a sandwich. I nearly lost it when she took the bread out and put it on the kitchen table.

"Oh baby..." I screamed grabbing the bread and a dishrag at the same time, "let momma wash that table."

Janiah stood in the center of the room, looking confused. "Mom… what are you talking about? The table isn't dirty," she said staring it.

"Well…. the landlord changed the light fixture today… and spilled some stuff on the table."

"Mom you tripping…"

If this table could talk—oh, the story it would tell. It would say… "Girl… your mama's legs was spread from Beverly Hills to Long Beach this morning. You better let this ho clean off this table."

"You know next weekend I have college orientation, right?" "Oh yeah…" I said, "you sure it ain't this weekend?"

"Next weekend."

"Okay Janiah," I said, "call your Auntie Ducky and see if you can stay over there this weekend. I may be out of town."

"Where you going, mom?"

"I might be going to Atlanta with Trillion," I said, "but I'm not 100% sure yet."

"Okay mom…keep me posted…gotta hit the books," she said slipping away into her bedroom to study. That night I had to make a decision on the weekend, so I called Luke hoping just to hear his voice and at the same time get some direction.

"Hello," he said in that deep, sexy voice. "Hi Luke…how you doing?" I asked. "I'm fine sexy," he said, "and how are you?" "Good…" I said starting to melt.

"I was just thinking about you," he said. "Really?"

"Yes really…" he said.

"What were you thinking?" I prodded.

"I was just thinking how much I like you…you remind me so much of my mother."

"Really?"

"You have the spirit of an angel," he said, "and that's just what my mother was to me."

Okay, I thought to myself. *There's no way in hell he would EVER meet Juicy.*

The angel reference would be quickly replaced with the live living devil.

"I feel the same way about you Luke. There's something very special about you, too."

"Thank you," he acknowledged.

"Luke, what are you doing this weekend?"

"I got to make a run to Vegas…business." Silence.

I was waiting for him to ask me to go.

That would be the perfect excuse to get me out of the Atlanta trip.

"So I'll call you when I get back?" he asked.

My heart dropped a bit. I had to admit I was disappointed for two reasons:

1. That I was NOT going to be with him in Vegas;

2. That I was GOING to be with Trillion and Chance in Atlanta.

"Sure," I said trying to sound like a trooper, "I hope you have a great trip."

"It's all business, baby…" he said offering me reassurance, "the second I get back I'm going to come see you."

Damn, I thought to myself when I hung up the phone. *Atlanta it is.*

chapter

19

I DON'T KNOW HOW IT happened because it happened so fast. One minute I was at home kissing my daughter goodnight, and the next minute I was on the pole at Luke's strip club.

What the hell?

It was a free-for-all.

Girls were rubbing on me, and I was rubbing on them. Before I could catch myself, I was down on my knees in the back office sucking the manager's dick.

What the hell?

Two minutes later, Luke busted the door open and I looked up at him with my eyes wide open and my mouth even wider.

Uh oh.

And that's when I woke up in a cold sweat. I was panting and moaning. Obviously, that would be the worst-case scenario. Thank God it was just a dream but it also made me realize that I wasn't ready to be in a committed relationship without knowing for sure that I was free of Juicy. I was left with no other choice but to back up and do the "moonwalk" out of this one.

In between all of this night and daydreaming, Janiah knocked on the door bringing my attention back to what was really going on.

"Mommy…I'm on my way to school." "Okay baby…I am going to Atlanta. Did you call your Aunt Ducky?"

"Yes…I'll go over to auntie's house after school." "Good."

"Mommy…you going to a party in Atlanta?" "No…you little nosy bitch. Why do you ask?"

"Auntie Ducky said you and the "B" was going to the All Star Game."

"What?" I asked, "don't pay your Auntie no attention…we're going to a business meeting."

"Business meeting?"

"Yes Janiah… I didn't even know the All Star Game was in Atlanta…. really?"

"Okay momma…" said Janiah rolling her eyes, "whatever you guys do just be safe and have fun," she said sarcastically.

"Okay my little lawyer," I said kissing her forehead. "Don't forget your keys."

When Janiah left I realized I was running short on time and I hadn't finished packing yet.

"Damn!" I said jumping out of bed grabbing everything I owned in my closet. I had to pull out my toughest outfits…I started pulling out my Gucci shoes, my Gucci purse, Gucci outfit, my Gucci swimsuits and Gucci hat.

I rarely pulled out my good stuff but growing up with a mother like Ida Mae, I have definitely purchased my share of the good stuff over the years. I nearly jumped out of my skin when the phone started ringing and I saw it was Trillion.

"Shit!" I said…"I hope she's not on her way…"

Ring.

Ring.

Ring.

"Hey girl!" I said, trying to sound already packed, waiting and bored.

"Hey lady….you ready?" Trillion asked.

"Where you at?" I asked hoping that she hadn't left the house yet.

"I'm outside…come on out…"

What? "Oooohhh," I said.

"You're not ready are you?" she asked disappointed. Silence.

"Mia!!!!"

"I'm sorry…just give me 30 minutes," I said, knowing I needed more like an hour.

"Damnit…." said Trillion, "all right…I need to call Chance anyway and see where she's at."

"I'll hurry," I promised.

When I got off the phone, I opened my bedroom curtain and could see Trillion's face all frowned-up, as she blabbed away on the phone to that damn Chance.

"Damn," I said, "I hope that phony, sharp-dressing heifer don't show."

Back in the day, Chance had some bad ass clothes and some bad ass, big, perky titties. Next to the "mouth piece" those big titties were her trademark. All the guys loved Chance's titties…and so did the girls. They all wished they had their own pair.

If I got a Juicy in the back then Chance certainly had two Juicy's in the front and if those titties were anything like my booty, Trillion better watch out. But I'm not worried about it…Juicy is long gone…at least I pray she is.

I couldn't help but notice how aggravated Trillion looked sitting in her car on the phone…she smiled at me, but I could still see she was pissed. I felt a vibe like she and Chance were talking about me, in a not-too-nice-kind of way…

Little did I know…

"Girl," said Trillion sitting inside of her car staring at Mia through the bedroom window, "this bitch got me sitting in my car waiting on her late ass."

"That's fucked up…I'd leave her ass," said Chance. "I know right…"

"Does that bitch still have that bad ass body…and don't know what to do with it?"

"Yeah," she said with a frown, "she's still built like a shit brick house…but that booty has gotten bigger!"

"Get the hell out!" "Seriously big…"

"Is she still that stuck-up, snobby bitch that still thinks she's too good for everybody?" asked Chance.

"Basically," said Trillion, "but there's another whole side to Mia."

"What? She on that pipe?"

"No, she more on that bottle…you'll see her this weekend," said Trillion. "She's a freak for real. She's just like us but don't know it. Just don't forget to bring those pills."

"I won't forget," promised Chance.

❧

The flight was long and Trillion and I both slept most of the way.

I was feeling a bit edgy and not completely at ease with the weekend. I was about to experience the world that I left not so long ago. I hadn't been in an environment where people were drinking and partying in months. But there was another part of me that needed to know that I had conquered the demon inside of me or have I?

Time would tell.

This weekend would tell. Liquor would tell.

And Trillion would tell…

"You alright?" Trillion asked as we waited on the corner to catch our cab to the Ritz.

"I'm good," I responded quickly, wanting to turn around and ask her if she really had my back because I was scared as hell.

"Welcome to the Hot ATL!" said Trillion, "I guess we're gonna turn into a couple of peaches right about now."

I laughed.

"Girl…this is the big booty capital of the world," said Trillion.

"For real?"

"Yeah girl…you ever heard of Magic City?"

"Magic City?"

"It's the most popular strip club in Atlanta…the booty's in there are like magic…they're unbelievably big."

"Why you doing all this booty talk with me?" I asked with irritation in my voice.

"Lighten up, Mia…you always thinking somebody's judging your booty."

I turned my back to Trillion for a minute to squash the conversation.

"I ain't thinking about your ass…I brought my own booty panties!" as Trillion turned around and shook her plump booty in Mia's face.

"Oh my God! Look at your booty!!" I said almost bursting into laughter.

"Bitch you ain't the only one who's gonna have booty in the booty capital of ATL!" said Trillion.

"I can't believe you, girl," they said as they got in the cab and sped off toward the Ritz.

❧

By the time we got to the room, Chance had already arrived and had cracked open the mini-bar. When Trillion and I walked into the room the first thing Chance did was open her arms to greet me as though we were long lost lovers.

"Mia!" she squealed in a high pitched voice, "how you doing? It's been years…and you still got that damn body. Is that ass ever going to shrink?"

"I told you girl!" cackled Trillion.

"Look at you Chance," said Mia, "I can't believe those titties haven't deflated! Looks like life has been good to you."

"Life has been great to me!" said Chance raising her drink into the air while making a toast, "to life!"

"Where's my drink?" asked Trillion making her way to the mini-bar as Mia observed Trillion and Chance with eyes of disappointment.

"Come on girl," said Chance, "have a drink!"

"No girl…I'm in recovery," I said.

"Don't let that get in the way…" suggested Chance raising another drink. "We're about to hit the biggest baller party in the ATL. There's going to be rappers, ballers, celebrities, everybody's on the guest list! So just relax…and have a drink…"

"No," said Trillion with a slight buzz, "my girl really can't take no drink."

"Suit yourself," said Chance as she slipped away into the bathroom, giving me an opportunity to address Trillion's behavior.

"What are you doing?" I asked, staring at Trillion with hard eyes.

"What are you talking about?" asked Trillion with attitude and another drink going down.

"I thought you had my back. I feel like I'm being put in an awkward position."

Trillion stared at me with blank eyes, and I could tell that she was slowly easing her way out of her promise to me.

"Maybe I should just go and you and Chance take this weekend to do what you do…"

"Don't be silly, Mia," said Trillion putting her arm around me, "you're my best friend…I won't let anything happen to you."

"Okay," I said trying to relax a bit, all the while noticing Trillion getting more and more intoxicated.

It was not a good look, for sure.

But I'm here…so I might as well have as much fun as I can.

So let me get sharp as hell and pull out my Gucci shoes, Gucci purse, Gucci suit and Gucci watch.

"Damn! You're a walking billboard for Gucci…what the fuck?" asked a drunk Chance, as we arrived at the party.

"You're one Gucci-dressing bitch!" screamed Trillion.

I was a little embarrassed as we made our way through the crowds of people that were waiting to get into the party. But with our VIP status and my Gucci apparel, we bypassed all lines.

"Shake your ass…shake your ass," said Trillion as we moved to the front of the line. "Work them titties…work them titties…" she said to Chance.

I was switching a real booty. Chance was jiggling real titties.

And Trillion was shaking a make-believe booty with all kinds of attitude.

"Step to the side boys," said Trillion as she rubbed her padded ass against some real hard dicks.

Trillion was tripping.

I had never seen her act so aggressive and overly excited. Guess she was a real groupie after all.

I just looked at her and shook my head as Trillion and Chance dipped into the bathroom and left me standing at the bar alone— easy prey for all the men who were foaming at the mouth, admiring my backside. I suddenly felt like it was "open season" on my booty and that my girls had ditched me—leaving me to fend for myself with a pack of wolves.

Welcome to Atlanta, I said to myself ordering a Club soda.

Meanwhile…

Trillion and Chance were standing in line to use the restroom.

"Between the perfume smell, underarm musk, funky koochie odor and weed smell, I might just fall out up in here," said Trillion.

"Girl, I know what you mean…I was wondering if that was your koochie smelling like that."

Trillion hits Chance in the arm, "shut up! I am NOT that funky… I douched twice today."

"I know that's right!"

"So you brought the ecstasy, right?" Trillion asked. "Hell yeah! I don't leave home without it."

"Give me one now. I want to get freaky tonight," insisted Trillion.

Chance reached in her purse and gave Trillion a handful of tiny pills.

"Fuck the old saying w*hat happens in Vegas stays in Vegas,"* boasted

Trillion, "we got a new saying...*no one tells what goes down in the ATL.*"

"Hey...what about your girl, Mia? She still seems stuck up and shit," Chance said.

"That's what I wanted to talk to you about. Mia is one sick cookie... she has another side to her that you would absolutely love."

"What you saying?"

"Girl, if I tried to tell you about Mia's crazy world you wouldn't believe me...so I have to show you."

"Come on...come on..." Chance bursts with anxiety-like enthusiasm. "What the fuck you talking about?"

"Chance, she got a booty on her..."

"Oh bitch please...tell me something I don't know."

"No serious...you don't know what I'm saying to you...her booty has its own personality and its own name."

"Get the fuck out!" screamed Chance. "You sound like the sick cookie to me..."

"No for real...her booty's name is Juicy and it talks!"

"How many of them mother fucking pills have you taken?" Chance asked, trying to pry my hand open.

"This booty is just like us..." promised Trillion, "it loves to fuck and suck, and suck and fuck."

"Is Mia an undercover slut like us?" Chance asked with child-like enthusiasm.

"No bitch...not Mia...but her booty Juicy is a straight ho!"

Chance stopped and looked hard at Trillion holding her hand out. "Give me back those pills."

"Forget you," said Trillion, "Come on...let's go get her. You'll see."

chapter

20

$\mathscr{I}$ WAS STARTING TO GET a dull ache in my left ear because the music was so loud. Just when I was about to get up and leave the bar, I caught sight of Trillion and Chance coming out of the bathroom. Both of those heifers looked tore up from where I stood, but they didn't know it.

What the hell took them so long? I couldn't help but wonder.

I felt like I was all by myself. I was so tired of every Niggah in here sending me drinks. I felt like I was at the ballpark "catching drinks" as fast as they could throw them at me. And every time I caught one, I said…

No thank you.

No thank you.

No thank you.

"No thank you," became my evening sermon.

The last drink that I was just about to reject, was caught on an interception—

"Thank you," said Trillion rudely interrupting my last "no thank you" for the night.

"What the hell took you so long?" Mia asked them.

"Girl…it was high drama in the bathroom…one of Chance's bra straps broke and I had to intervene before one of those titties fall on the floor and cause some structural damage in the building."

"Did you fix it?" I asked laughing.

"Yeah," said Trillion, "glad I had a box of safety pins."

"I was starting to get worried…I thought you guys left me here with these heathens."

"These Niggah's up in here ain't no heathens! I wouldn't give a damn if you guys left me here in this goldmine by myself," Chance said.

"Chance, you are still the same," said Mia with a fake smile, thinking to herself—*age ain't changed this ho a bit!!*

"You still the same, too," said Chance with an equally fake smile, thinking to herself—*you the biggest undercover ho in the room!!*

Baby Got Back by Sir Mix A Lot starts pumping through the speakers and bouncing off the walls.

"This is my favorite song!" screamed Trillion as her drunk ass started dancing at the bar.

"I don't know why this is your favorite song…you don't have no back. That should be Mia's favorite song."

I started to laugh, but it wasn't a real laugh because I really wasn't feeling them. I was just sitting here questioning why I came in the first place. I would have much preferred to spend the weekend with Luke in Vegas. I was also getting a weird vibe from them, that I wasn't part of the team. Maybe this was the part of the group that I outgrew. At long last, I was finally starting to love me and discover through my friendship with Luke—that someone *could* actually like me for me and not judge me. I didn't feel a desire to drink or participate in any of the festivities. The whole scene seemed unnatural—everyone was trying to cover up who they really were with all the perpetrators and wanna-be's.

Everyone was playing their part. All characters in a drama.

The stage was set.

The dialogue predictable.

The actors already had their scripted lines—and I knew what they were going to say before they said it.

So what do you do?

I'm a rapper.

A ball player.

Music producer.
OR
A model.
A+ plus actress,
A video girl.
Broke and a wanna-be...
Oh that's the part they leave out.
So what do you drive?
Ferrari.
Mercedes.
Porsche.
I rented it for the All-Star Weekend.
But that's another part they leave out.

Oh, the parts we play to be accepted, to be appreciated, to be wanted and loved.

I no longer wanted to be a part of the business. I wasn't interested in taking on any more roles.

By now, both of my ears were hurting and I couldn't take it anymore.

"Trillion," I asked when she finally stopped dancing to Sir Mix-A-Lot's song…"you got any aspirin? My head is killing me."

Trillion's eyes lit up.

"Yeah," she said, giving Chance "the look." Chance's eyes widened. She knew that look.

"Oh yeah," said Chance, nodding her head slowly.

Mia laid her head on the counter for a moment, and Trillion winked at Chance as she pulled out the ecstasy pill.

"Take two of these…" insisted Trillion, "and your headache will be gone in a second."

Mia accepted the "pills" and Chance immediately offered "her" a drink but Mia quickly rejected it. "No thank you."

"You're such a dud," said Chance rolling her eyes.

As Mia swallowed the pills with a glass of water, Trillion quietly mouthed the words to Chance…*watch this.*

Trillion and Chance started dancing and grinding on each other. Trillion was grabbing Chance's titties, Chance was playing with Trillion's hair and I started getting very nauseous. The whole room started spinning and I felt like I was about to throw up. I quickly started moving toward the bathroom, but Trillion grabbed my arm and with a big smirk on her face blurted, "What's wrong, Mia? Starting to leave us?"

Chance and Trillion both started laughing. Chance gave Trillion a high five and I knew in that moment I had been set up.

chapter

21

I RAN AS FAST AS I COULD to the bathroom, slamming into women and almost knocking them over. One woman spilled a drink and damn near fell on the floor I sideswiped her so hard. But I didn't care, all I was trying to do was make it to the bathroom before I threw up all on the floor. I felt as though I was in the fight for my life—and I could feel myself beginning to slip away.

But why?

I didn't have anything to drink, but the "aspirin" Trillion gave me must have been drugs.

Oh God, I thought to myself, *I need to get out here.* But I didn't know where to go and who to trust.

I cut through the bathroom line and busted right into the next available stall. I didn't even close the door behind me—I simply dropped to my knees and began throwing up in the toilet, praying that I would not surrender to the devil that was rising up within me. Slowly, I began to stand up but before I could turn around, someone was tapping me on the shoulder.

"Excuse me," said a short, thin woman wearing a mini-skirt and five-inch platforms, "but you just damn near knocked me down. You spilled my drink on the floor. What do you have to say for yourself?"

"Well excuse me, Bitch! I'm sorry…I guess I have to whoop your ass!"

The woman's eyes bucked out of her head.

"Do you know who the fuck I am?" the woman asked, rearing her neck back.

"Hell naw, Bitch. Do you know who the fuck I am? I'm Juicy, Bitch."

The woman backed away from the stall, intimated by Juicy's wild-looking eyes.

"You stay right here…" the woman said to Juicy, "I'm going to get security to escort you out of this party. You're rude and do not belong here. I'll be right back."

"Okay," said Juicy, shrugging her shoulders. "I'll be right back too… I need to go get a drink."

Juicy came out of the stall with all eyes are on her, but she didn't give a damn. Unfazed, she walked to the mirror, put some red lipstick on, pushed those titties up and turned around in the mirror and stared at herself—rubbing on the booty.

"You one fine bitch!" Juicy said, talking to herself in the mirror. "I love your mother fucking ass! Literally!"

She pat her booty.

"Let's go out here and get some dick and some cash…my two favorite words."

Juicy looked up in the mirror, and a heavy-set woman came up beside Juicy at the sink and sat her drink down. Juicy reached across the woman, picked up the woman's drink and guzzled it—while the woman looked on in absolute shock.

"Your fat ass knows what I'm talking about!" she said to the woman. "Dicks and cash…."

The woman was horrified and speechless.

Out of the corner of Juicy's eye, she noticed all of the other women in the crowded restroom staring at her in disbelief.

"What you bitches looking at?" she asked. "You bitches don't like fucking and sucking? I'm so tired of you self-righteous, fake ass, church-going ho's…be a real bitch like me."

Proud to suck dicks. Proud to fuck.

Proud to steal your money and your man. No one said a word. The room was speechless.

A few shake their head.

"Fuck all of you bitches," she said and walked out of the bathroom.

Once outside the bathroom, Juicy saw Trillion across the dance floor and shouted over the music, "TRILLION! TRILLION!" she shouted walking toward Trillion.

"What's up hookers?" Juicy said to Trillion and Chance, "these bitches are tripping up in here!"

Chance shot one eye to Trillion and shook her head in disbelief, "Hell no! Who the fuck is this?"

"I'm Juicy, Bitch," Juicy said to Chance.

"Juicy's bbaaaaaaaaaaaccccckkkkk!" Trillion laughed.

"She looks like Mia…but she don't talk, walk or act like Mia!" Chance said, still in absolute shock.

Juicy eyeballs Chance. "So, you the Bitch Mia and Trillion been dogging out."

Trillion chokes up for a minute.

"Just playing, bitch…" Juicy said, "Mia don't give a fuck about me either. Fuck that square bitch. We going to have some fun tonight."

"Juicy, I'm so glad to see you again," said Trillion.

"Hey, we might have to fight some bitches tonight. You ho's, down with me?"

"Hell yeah," said Trillion.

Chance continues to look on in utter amazement.

"You bitches knew I was coming to the party…so where's my mother fucking drink?"

"Girl…I got you a whole bottle of your favorite poison… Vodka!" screams Trillion.

"You my kind of ho!" said Juicy accepting the bottle of Vodka and downing it right there at the bar with no glass.

"These guys have been sending the *other* you drinks all night, but you weren't accepting them."

"Yeah I know," said Juicy, "that Bitch thought she had gotten rid of me…I was kind of worried for a minute but this time, I'm not going back in."

"What you saying?" Trillion asked. "That shit ya'll gave Mia knocked her the fuck out. I feel stronger than I've ever felt. I might even be strong enough to finally take over this body for good."

Chance came out of shock-zone and began to question Juicy. "So where did Mia go?"

"Mia's gone bye bye….and I'm Juicy…Mia's talking booty." "Why are you here?" Chance inquired.

Juicy went on to explain.

"I'm Mia's confidence…I love me. Mia just never understood me. I really wish she could see all of the attention we get in this world. She would have been a millionaire if she would have listened to me in the bathroom years ago. All the dumb bitch would have had to do was to stay high and allow me to run this show."

"Girl…I like you…you are cool as hell! I like your ass much better than that stuck up Bitch, Mia."

"I like those nice set of titties on you," said Juicy, "I'd like to suck on 'em one day!"

Chance and Trillion laughed.

"Where did you come from, Juicy?" Chance continued with her line of questioning.

"I was created by that greedy bitch, Ida Mae." "Mia's mother?" Trillion asked surprised.

"I always lived in Mia's subconscious mind. Like I said, Ida Mae put me there," said Juicy as she guzzled the last drop of Vodka in the bottle. "But remember this, you black ass ho's…whatever you program your kids to be in this fucked up world they will be it one way or another. Even if they hate it or hate you."

"Damn! You're kind of deep, Juicy…" Chance said. "Fuck all that… get me another bottle of Vodka." Trillion laughed.

"I'll tell you stank bitches something else…that stupid bitch Mia hates me so much….but I bet if she took her ass outside without me— imagine all of the attention she *wouldn't* get. And one day, it will stop because the bitch is getting old and I'll get tired of sitting up so straight on that bitch's back! I will start to deflate and then what will her old ass do?"

Trillion and Chance almost fell out on the floor they were laughing so hard.

"But the retard sure does know how to dress me…she loves to wear those tight ass jeans and I love how she shows me off!"

"Girl…me and you are so much alike…I love your ass Juicy," said Chance. "Tell me some more…"

"Am I getting paid for this mother fucking interview? Enough of this. You broke bitches smelling what I'm smelling?" she asked, sniffing across the bar.

"What you smelling?" asked Trillion.

"I'm smelling some green dollar bills burning up in these Niggah's pockets up in here."

"Oh yes…" said Chance nodding her head, "I'm definitely smelling that!"

"Bitches…this is what I call the Baller Alert!" said Juicy. "Those money looking Niggah's over there in the corner have been staring at us all night," said Chance.

"Yeah, ho…I recognize that," said Juicy. "I been staring at those Niggah's pants and pockets for the last hour."

"Why were you staring at his pants? I can understand the pockets…but the pants?" Chance asked.

"I been checking out the pants, you stupid bitch to see who's got the biggest dick up in here!"

"Juicy, you are fucking crazy!" blurted Trillion.

Juicy started scoping the place out. She spotted a guy with a Valentino suit, diamond cuff links, Rolex watch, and two, studded diamond earrings. She couldn't help but notice that he also had a rock on his finger that could blind you from ten miles away.

Juicy's pupils disappeared and were instantly replaced by green dollar bill signs.

"Juicy…" said Trillion, "I never knew you had green eyes."

But Juicy paid them no mind—she was already en route across the room to the bling, bling man. As she approached, he smiled at her. He looked like a fine ass Puerto Rican. Standing 6'4 inches, he was so sexy it would have been impossible to resist.

"Hello," he said extending a hand to Juicy, who was followed by Chance and Trillion. "My name is Keno."

"Hi…my name is Juicy," said Juicy as she slowly turned around to give him a front view of the backside. At the same time, both Trillion and Chance reached across Juicy to introduce themselves.

I'm Trillion.

I'm Chance.

"Back up…you stank bitches," said Juicy under her breath to the girls.

As Keno took in the whole scene, he appreciated each of the girls for their unique gifts. His eyes fell from Trillion's beautiful face, to Chance's outrageous titties to Juicy's gigantic booty.

"This feels like paradise, ladies," he said with a smile, pointing to each girl. "Why do they call you Trillion? You Chance and you Juicy?"

"I'm Trillion because I'm worth more than a million."

"I'm Chance, mother fucker, because I'm your last Chance to experience heaven on earth," she said pressing her titties against him.

"And they call me Juicy cause my pussy's tight and Juicy!"

"Well," he said licking his lips, "all of this sounds so delicious.

I'd like to introduce you ladies to my boy, Bernard."

"Yeah…" said Juicy, "I been waiting on an introduction. Your friend has been staring at my ass all night. One is fun but two, I can definitely do."

"Do what?" Bernard asked, coming in on the tail end of the conversation.

"Oh…he's an ass man for sure," said Keno, "he's the one been sending you drinks all night."

All eyes turned to Bernard, the ass man. He was fine as hell. Standing 6'2 with strong, muscular arms, he wore a silk shirt that laid like fine carpet against his chocolate skin. He boasted a Gucci shirt, Gucci shoes, and a Gucci watch with a big diamond chain around his neck. He, too, wore large diamond studs in both ears. As Juicy was calculating the net worth of Keno and Bernard's jewelry alone, she was running numbers through her head like an automatic cash register—registering about half a million dollars. "So what kind of business are you guys in?" Trillion asked.

"We play ball," Keno said.

Juicy sidekicks Chance and whispers under her breath, "Jackpot, Bitch!"

Just then Biggie's song blasts through the speakers.

"I love it when you call me Big Papa!" said Trillion, who starts dancing with herself right there in the middle of the floor.

"You guys wanna dance?" Bernard asked Trillion and Chance, pulling them on to the crowded dance floor.

"You wanna dance Big Papa?" Juicy asked Keno.

He smiled and within seconds Juicy grabbed Keno's hand and drags him to the dance floor. Juicy started dancing real sexy-like, all over Keno. Juicy was shaking that booty, making it pop and rubbing her booty on Keno's dick. The more she rubbed, the harder he got. Juicy actually turned around, grabbed his dick on the dance floor, and whispered into his ear, "Let me suck it…"

Keno's eyes widened. He was caught between excitement and shock.

"You always so raw?" he asked Juicy. "You ain't seen shit yet…"

Keno was getting so excited that his dick was sticking out of his pants as he turned Juicy's big booty around on his dick and tried to put it up in her right on the dance floor. When she turned around, Juicy could see that Trillion and Chance were grinding on Bernard and each other—as they took turns dancing between his legs. Eventually, the music switched from fast to slow, and this is when Juicy made a big move. It was so crowded on the dance floor that Juicy and Keno were pressed against each other. Juicy started rubbing all over herself. She was licking her fingers and putting them inside of Keno's mouth.

"You want some of this?" she asked.

By this time, Keno was in a daze. Juicy put her hands down inside of his pants rubbing all around the tip of his dick. She started to lick all in between his ears then Juicy whispered into his ear.

"Keno…you can have all of me from the back to the front." He looked like he was about to pass out.

"I will suck that big dick until you cum all in my mouth."

He wanted to explode as Juicy kept massaging his dick up and down.

"How much would you pay to have this pussy and this asshole?"

On the verge of explosion, all that he could say was "whatever you like."

That was all greedy Juicy needed to hear. She damn near gave him whiplash pulling him off the dance floor. She hit Trillion and Chance in the arm and said, "Let's go you tired bitches…we going back to the room."

"What's up?" Trillion asked.

"Bring the other Niggah, too, and let's get the fuck on," commanded Juicy.

Within minutes, Keno, Bernard, Trillion and Chance were all following commando Juicy like a puppy on a leash. She was running things.

"Get five mo!" Juicy said to Trillion. "Five mo' what?" Trillion asked.

"Five more bottles of Vodka, you dumb Bitch…and get something for ya'll to drink!" Juicy screamed.

As they headed out the door, Trillion and Chance pulled Bernard into their rented Mercedes and Keno jumped in his Maserati. Juicy dripped an extra drop of "koochie juice" when saw the Maserati that Keno was driving.

"It's on," said Juicy. "The bitch is gone."

"What Bitch?" he asked as she slid into the front seat. "Mia…"

"Who's Mia?"

"She was an old friend of mine that just passed away," she said with a laugh.

"And that's who you just called a bitch…your friend that died?"

"It's a long story…don't worry about it," she said, as she put her hand on his dick. "Just give me some of that baby juice."

"What baby juice?" he asked, trying to drive. "That juice that comes from your dick."

Keno was tripping but his dick kept getting harder and harder as Juicy unzipped his pants and pulled his dick out, bent down, and started to suck every bit of his juice out. Within minutes, Keno came all over Juicy's face. Juicy swallowed every ounce of it up. Keno was trying his best to drive right but he lost control for a quick moment and the car swerved to the side. He pulled the car over and stopped a moment to clean himself up, but this time, Juicy took complete control.

"Baby…let me drive so you can get rest 'cause we'll be right back at this real soon."

"Shit," he said, barely able to move. "Where you been all of my life?"

They switched seats and Juicy sped off like a maniac. Within seconds, they pulled up to the hotel right behind Chance and Trillion's rented Mercedes, which was already parked. When the valet guy opened the door, Juicy's dress was up around her hips and she had no panties on.

"Excuse me!" yelled the valet, as he jumped back in embarrassment.

"Excuse you for what?" Juicy asked.

His eyes dropped to her bare koochie, and following his eyes, she looked down and saw what he saw.

"At least my shit don't stink," she said, jumping out of the car with cum on her face, as she waited for a groggy Keno to get out of the car.

Come on you slow ass motha fucker, she said to herself, eyeballing his $100,000 Rolex.

Once Juicy and Keno made it to the elevator, Juicy was on her knees again unzipping Keno's pants.

"Hold it, baby," said Keno, "let's get to the room!" "Okay baby..." said Juicy getting off her knees.

They rode to the 30th floor and exited the elevator together. Once they made it to the room, Juicy banged on the door as hard as she could.

"Open up the door, sluts!" she demanded.

Within moments, the door slowly opened to reveal a naked Trillion.

"Hell yeah, Trillion! I see why you're worth a million!" blurted Keno.

When they entered, Trillion pulled Juicy to the side and gave her some more ecstasy pills.

"Hey girl...take some more of these pills," said Trillion. Juicy eagerly accepts.

"And don't forget a little something to wash it down with," Trillion said handing her another bottle of Vodka.

Trillion knew that Juicy needed to stay high because if the high wore off and Mia came out—the party would be over.

"Good looking out, Bitch..." said Juicy. "Now back up off my dick, trick" pushing Trillion to the side, "I'm going to finish sucking this lollipop—you better go find yours."

It was obvious by the look on Keno's lit up face that he wanted to fuck both of them, but he didn't want any catfights to break out. He spotted Bernard coming out of the room and by Bernard's tired face, it looked like he was already fucked out. Keno said, "damn niggah... what the fuck you been doing?"

"Man these two freaks up in here are turning me the fuck out," said Bernard taking a seat on the couch. "Your turn."

As Keno glanced around the room, he was amazed by what he saw. This fabulous suite was a disaster. Lamps were over-turned and pictures that were hanging on the wall were now on the floor. Several of the couch pillows were scattered throughout the hallway and liquor bottles and lines of coke were lying on the table.

"Oh...my kind of party," squealed Juicy, as she dropped to her knees and snorted a line of coke. She motioned for Keno to join her, and once he dropped to his knees, she shoved his head down into the coke. He almost caught whiplash she pushed his neck down so hard.

"Come on motha fucker…I need to get that dick back in full operation! Snort up!"

Juicy surveyed the room and walked into the master suite, followed closely by Keno. Keno's eyes widened with surprise when he saw a big Jacuzzi sitting right in the middle of the floor filled to the top with bubbles and a butt-naked Chance playing with herself. As he glanced around the room, he was mesmerized by the multiple reflections of Chance masturbating in all of the images around him. It was like watching a hundred small screen TV sets—all broadcasting the same freak show.

"Damn!" he said, mouth wide open.

Chance was fixated on the bulge between Keno's legs. She was licking her lips and staring him down. Keno was equally as interested in her.

"Juicy, can I have some?" Chance asked Juicy.

"Yeah bitch, but let me get this dick ready for us," replied Juicy as she unzipped his pants and took her top off at the same time. Keno was helping her out of her pants and her panties.

"Hey baby," she said unsnapping Keno's Rolex, "let me get this for you…we can't get this expensive shit wet."

"Yeah…Yeah…" he said, oblivious to the fact that she removed the watch and deposited it into her purse, which was stationed nearby. She then proceeded to lick his neck and caress his earlobes with her tongue—which made him moan, and overlook the fact that she had sucked the 5-carat studs right off his ears and into her mouth, before spitting them out into her hand.

"Yeah baby…" he moaned, lost in the moment.

"You like that?" Juicy asked, making her way around to all of his worldly possessions, including his wallet and diamond belt buckle, which all ended up in her oversized purse, along with the Rolex and the diamond earrings. But Keno didn't know the difference—he was so caught up in the images in the mirror of Chance, who was on her way to a real nice orgasm. It couldn't have been a better distraction.

"Hey Keno," said Chance interrupting her flow, "come over here and let me see if I can hide that big dick between my titties." "Baby... with all those titties you got...you could lose about ten dicks in there!" Chance laughed.

"Shut the fuck up," said Juicy irritated, "let me suck on those big titties and that big dick," she said sliding into the Jacuzzi, pulling Keno with her.

Once Juicy sunk into the water, she lunged toward Chance and grabbed one of her titties, and Keno grabbed the other. They were sucking like they were breastfeeding on Chance's titties.

"Damn..." hollered Chance. "Hold up! That hurts!"

Juicy let go of Chance's titties, dunked her head underwater and started sucking Keno's dick.

Juicy was sucking and stroking.

Keno and Chance were screaming and shouting.

Juicy came up for air and then went back down like an oral submarine. She switched teams and it was Chance's turn. She pulled Chance's legs apart and sucked Chance dry underwater. Chance could barely contain her pleasure, and she slowly immersed herself underwater and dived into Juicy's pussy.

Juicy exploded to the top of the water, coming up again for air, as she pushed Chance away hard. Chance, too, came up.

"Wait a minute, Bitch! I do the sucking and fucking up in here!" said Juicy.

Interrupting the cat squabble, Keno grabbed Juicy by the hair and turned her around.

"Give me some of that fat ass!" he demanded. "Hell yeah...." said Juicy, "my favorite position."

As Juicy got into position, Keno pulled Chance by the hair and flipped her into the same position. He had them both perched over the Jacuzzi like two dogs in heat and was hitting them from the back—hard as hell.

Chance was screaming—suspended somewhere between pain and pleasure. But for Juicy, it was straight pleasure.

"Harder! Harder!" screamed Juicy. "Ease up...ease up!" demanded Chance. "I don't feel shit!" screamed Juicy.

"You tearing up my pussy!" said Chance.

Juicy was fucking Keno back so hard that he stopped and turned her around just to stare at her.

"You are a BEAST!" he said.

"I'm every man's animal," Juicy said with a smile.

Chance was grateful for the "pause" as she climbed out of the tub and collapsed onto the floor, unable to move.

Juicy just looked at Chance and shook her head. In the background, she could hear Trillion screaming like a wounded dog. Juicy shouted over the loud screams of Trillion, who was entertaining Bernard in the front room, "Bitch...if you can't handle that dick bring it in here!"

"This party sounds better than our party!" said Trillion, as she and Bernard joined the group.

She immediately got off Keno's dick and moved towards Bernard's dick.

"Come on in here..." said Juicy who was so excited to see him, she couldn't stop staring and shaking. She almost came again—at the sight of his Rolex, diamond ring and necklace still blinging into the mirror.

Juicy tuned out everyone in the room and focused intently on Bernard and his jewelry.

"Come over here, baby," she said, opening her arms to him. "This shit is too expensive to get wet...let me help you out of this shit."

Like a puppy dog, he quickly responded and hopped in the Jacuzzi where he quickly grabbed her ass, meeting her with a massive erection. She started kissing his neck and skillfully unlocked the necklace, dropping the diamond beneath her tongue. Next, she went for the earlobes, and much like Keno, he was moaning and lost in the experience.

Too bad....because she just made off with diamond earrings. In the meantime, Keno and Trillion were going at it, while Chance lay passed out on the floor.

"Let's get this out of the way," she said—taking off the Rolex and tossing it across the room—into her favorite purse.

To make certain that his mind did not return to his possessions, she dropped beneath the water and went to town on his dick, as Bernard nearly explodes. He pulled her up out of the water, flipped her onto the floor and started to hit it from the back.

"More! More!" she screamed.

Harder!

Harder!

By this time, Chance, Trillion and Keno are passed out on the floor.

Harder! Harder!

Juicy flipped Bernard on his back, climbed on top and started screaming!

Harder! Harder!

"Damn!" screamed Bernard. "You are an ANIMAL!" "I'm a beast to every man!" she said with a grin.

As Bernard began to cum, Juicy jumped off and put his dick into her mouth.

"Cum daddy!" she commanded. And he did.

Exploded right in her mouth.

Within seconds, Bernard was out cold.

Juicy sat up and looked at Trillion, Chance, Keno and Bernard all laid out unconscious.

"All weak bitches!" Juicy said, giving herself a high five, as she collected Bernard's wallet, Chance's earrings and Trillion's watch, stuffing them all into her bag. "I'm a bad motha fucker!"

chapter

22

*A*S THE SUN BEGAN to creep across the sky turning night to day, Juicy was still wide awake—and with nothing left to steal, drink or snort, she began to get sleepy *and* worried. She had never stayed out this long and was terrified to go to sleep lest Mia return and shut her down forever. Almost panic-stricken about her uncertain future, she ran to the living room and fell to the ground where she tried to snort the shadowy residue of leftover cocaine. But all she really got was a whiff of dust and debris. So much so, that she began coughing and choking on dust.

"God damn…all the dope is gone," Juicy cried out. "Greedy motha fuckers!"

She tried to take a swallow of Vodka, but all the scattered bottles of alcohol proved to be empty, dry containers—thanks to Juicy.

"Greedy motha fuckas!" she howled as she made her way to the bedroom where all the burned-out partygoers lay unconscious on the floor. Keno caught Juicy's eye as he lay sprawled on the bedroom floor with a gigantic morning erection.

Hhhhhmmmmm, Juicy thought.

No more dope.

No more liquor.

But there is plenty of dick left.

And with that, she dropped to her knees and began sucking Keno's dick. Slowly, Keno came to life, rousing from a deep sleep. "Baby… that feels so good," he moaned. "What a way to wake a Niggah up."

"Just shut the fuck up and give me some of that baby juice!" "Damn baby…what kind of drug you on?" he asked.

"I'm on that 'can't get enough dick drug,'" she said with a grin.

Keno's dick was more of a pacifier than anything else, because the more Juicy sucked the sleepier she got.

Weaker and weaker, she began to feel.

Sucking.

Sucking.

Sleeping.

Sucking.

Sleeping.

"Turn over baby…and take this dick!" Keno said.

Juicy couldn't wait to turn over because after all—that was her favorite position. And no sooner than she flipped on her stomach did Keno ram his morning erection inside of her.

"Hercules! Hercules!" she shouted as he banged her from the back. "Baby, you like all of this dick!"

Who's your daddy?

Who's your daddy?

You like this big black dick!

Take all of this dick!

Filled with confidence, Keno finally felt like he had put it down. Stud of the hour. Hercules.

Hercules.

"Who's your daddy?" he shouted. Silence.

And more silence.

"Who's your daddy, bitch?" he screamed on the verge of explosion.

Silence.

Silence.

Snoring.

Snoring.

Snoring.

"Wake up! I know you ass ain't gone to sleep on me!" he said, pulling her hair as his dick began to wilt. He snatched her by the hair, turning her over on her back, which shook Juicy awake. Keno slipped his dick in again and Juicy rocked her hips back and forth—fucking him back hard.

"Fuck me, daddy!" screamed Juicy. "Fuck me!" As Keno went to town, he heard another voice. "Get off me!" screamed Mia.

"Fuck me!" shouted Juicy.

"Get off!" panicked Mia.

"Deeper!" interrupted Juicy, as she struggles with Mia from the inside. "Don't stop! Keep fucking me! Keep fucking me!"

"Rape! Rape!" screamed Mia.

The mood was blown.

Sex over.

Keno jumped up and shouted, "What the fuck is wrong with you?"

Suddenly, Juicy's exterior walls began to soften and Mia began to cry. But only for a moment, then a hard Juicy makes a bitter frown on her face, and the soft look fades to rage. Juicy and Mia battle it out on the floor between the violent extremes of both worlds.

"Die bitch!" screamed Juicy, "this body belongs to me!" "Get out of me!" cried Mia. "Get out! Go away!"

"I'm not leaving, you Black Bitch!!" Juicy screamed. "Get away from me!" Mia screamed. "Help!!!!"

"I'm gonna kill you, Bitch!" Juicy screamed as she began to wilt, fade and bleed into the background. The drugs and alcohol are too far gone from Mia's body for Juicy to stay present. She cannot hold on any longer.

"You are a CRAZY, bitch!" said Keno.

Mia is back and horrified by what she sees. She bursts into tears as she takes it all in. There are naked bodies everywhere and Keno is standing over her—which intimates the hell out of her.

"What the fuck! Did you break out of a mental institution?" Keno shouted.

Rape!
Rape!
Rape!
Rape!

Mia's accusation echoes off the walls—bouncing through the room—waking the sleeping dead. Everyone is in a daze, utterly shocked, but Keno and Bernard are especially alarmed by the accusation.

Rape!
Rape!
Rape!

Keno cuts a look to Bernard.

"Let's get the fuck out of here! This Bitch is sick!!!!"

Bernard jumps up in a flash, snatches the closest pair of pants, which belong to Keno, and puts them on. Keno grabs Bernard's pants and puts them on.

"The fucking cops are coming!" screamed Bernard. "Let's roll!" Keno shouts.

In less than a minute, they are both out the door while Trillion and Chance both grab Mia and try to contain her hysterics.

"Mia! Mia! Mia!" screamed Trillion, "Calm down! Calm down! You're here with us!"

"It's okay!" said Chance, "let me get you something to drink."

Mia is lost in hysterics, as Chance pours a glass of water and hands it to Mia. Mia knocks the water clear across the room.

"What the fuck have you done to me!" screamed Mia. "How could you let this happen! I trusted you!"

Chance is as mesmerized by the transformation of Juicy to Mia as she was in seeing Mia turn to Juicy. *Wow!* she thinks to herself, this *bitch* really is crazy!

"Mia…you was the one doing all the fucking and sucking up in here!" said Chance. "Hell…you raped us, Bitch!"

Mia was so overcome with anger, that she was ready to fight

Chance—who didn't mind taking her on because they never did like each other. But Trillion stepped in because she knew it couldn't go down like that.

"You knew I couldn't drink!" shouted Mia.

"I didn't give you nothing to drink," defended Trillion, "Chance gave you some pills to loosen you up."

Chance shot Trillion a dirty look.

"Bitch please," Chance said to Trillion, "you the one told me this stupid ho had two personalities…and how I just had to see it."

Mia was furious and shot a look to Trillion. "Stop lying, Chance!" Trillion screamed.

"Trillion…you the one that said you hate this stuck-up Bitch, Mia…"

"I said no such thing!" defended Trillion as Mia looked on in shock.

"That's right…that's right," said Chance nodding her head.

"Trillion, you told me out of your own mouth that I would love Juicy because she was just like us!"

Mia gasped in horror.

In a rage, Mia quickly packed up her belongings.

Trillion followed on Mia's heels, apologizing and ass-kissing. "Mia…" said Trillion, "Please don't leave. Chance is tripping. She was drinking all night. She doesn't even know what she's saying…" "I know exactly what I'm saying," said Chance, "I'm saying exactly what you told me, yesterday!"

"I don't want to hear anymore!" screamed Mia… "just let me get my shit and I'm outta here."

Chance and Trillion went silent. No one spoke again.

"I'm sorry, Mia," Trillion said, but Mia threw up a single hand—which meant she didn't want to hear it—at all.

Mia grabbed her last bag and slammed the door of the hotel room, which shook the entire suite. Trillion and Chance exchanged 'dumbfounded' looks.

"That's your friend," said Chance. "You a dirty bitch."

"Fuck you!" said Trillion flipping her off.

"I ain't fucking with your tricky ass once we get back to L.A," declared Chance, "Hell, if Mia can't trust you...I know I can't trust you."

Suddenly, their bickering is interrupted by an unexpected hotel phone call.

They freeze in their tracks.

"Who could be calling?" Trillion asked. "Security!" said Chance, "all that damn screaming." "Shit!" said Trillion as she answered the phone.

"Hello maid service..." said Trillion with a fake Latin accent. "Hello???" said Keno on the other line.

"Hola..." said Trillion still faking it.

Chance is looking on with a confused look on her face, but Trillion simply fans her off, motioning for her to be quiet.

"I just left that room...have the girls who were staying there checked out?" Keno asked.

"Sí..." said Trillion. "No girls here."

"Motha fuck!" said Keno, "did you find some jewelry, watches, rings, wallets...is there anything left in the motha fucking room???"

"No sir...No one here. Me speak no English."

"Fuck!" said Keno to Bernard through the line, "these bitches ripped us off!"

"We gonna get those bitches!" Bernard's angry voice leaked through the phone line.

Trillion's eyes widened with fear, as Keno slammed the phone down.

"What?" Chance asks.

"We gotta get out of here," said Trillion, "Juicy robbed those Niggahs."

"What!" blurted Chance, "they don't have any way of getting in touch with you, right?

"Damn...I gave Bernard my business card...he's got all my contact info."

"Shit!" said Chance. "We gotta get back to L.A."

At the same time, Chance looked down at her own hand and notices her diamond ring missing. "Shit...Juicy got us, too."

Trillion noticed in that moment that her watch was missing too.

"At least our shit was fake...let's get the hell out of here!" confessed Chance.

"My shit wasn't fake, Bitch," protested Trillion.

"Yeah right!" said Chance, "I saw that same watch you were wearing downtown in the Alley for ten dollars, no tax."

"Fuck off!" said Trillion.

"Fuck you too...that's why I ain't fucking with your phony ass no more when we get back to L.A."

Mia walks out of the hotel and the moment she hit the curb, two taxicabs almost crash into each other, trying to get her attention.

"You need a cab!" a fat, greasy Black man with a sweaty forehead and big belly shouts.

"Yes," I said anxiously.

He jumped out and snatched her bag, throwing it in the back of the cab. He opened the door for her and she quickly jumped in.

"Where to?" he asked, taking his seat in the front seat. "Airport."

As the cab pulled off, I began to feel the weight of a heavy heart pressing against my chest. Filled with heavy regret and remorse, I knew deep down that Trillion was up to no good. I shook my head in disbelief. Obviously, Trillion and Chance did not have my best interests at heart.

I knew that I could not beat the beast that lived inside of me, and I also knew that I needed real help—psycho help. I also realized that I couldn't trust a soul. Growing more and more impatient with each mile, this began to feel like the longest ride in history. I was anxious and nervous and began to tap on the back of seat.

"Excuse me...how much longer to the airport?"

"Ten minutes," he said foaming at the mouth, "you trying to leave me so soon?"

"I got to catch the next thing smoking!"

"What's wrong?" he inquired. "Are you in trouble?" "Not yet," I said. "Not yet?"

"The longer I stay…the more trouble I might get into," I confessed. The cab driver laughed. I didn't.

I knew that there was a good possibility that I might be in some real trouble.

"What you do for a living?" he asked, "you a dancer?" "No!" I quickly responded. "I work in the family business."

"Does your family own a strip joint? Cause you look real familiar…"

I gasped.

"I'm not trying to be rude but you got a hell of a booty on you!" "Yeah," I responded with attitude, "but don't judge a booty by its cover."

"I'm not judging. I'm just admiring."

"Yeah…yeah….but it's exhausting to carry around in more ways than one," I said exasperated.

Within moments, the cab pulled up to the curb and came to a swift stop. Looking through the rear view mirror, the cabbie smiled at me and nodded his head, "Good luck to you, sweet peach!"

"Thanks," I said getting out of the cab, "I definitely need it."

I reached in my purse to pay the fare, but he immediately throws up one hand in protest, "No! No! No! This ride's on me."

I paused a beat.

"Thank you!" I said with a giant smile, which quickly faded when he opened up his big mouth and blurted, "You already paid me, darling…when you entered my cab and let me see all that ass!"

I frowned, slammed the door and headed straight to the ticket counter. All I could think about was going back to my family and new friend, Luke. I only prayed that what happened in the ATL no one would tell.

As I approached the reservations desk, the clerk behind the counter was slow to respond. She seemed to be lost in a fog or some sort of daze, as I waited to be acknowledged. The clerk was wearing a loud orange and green blouse with matching orange hair and gold teeth, smiling from ear to ear.

"May I help you, ma'am?" she finally asked.

"Yes. Are there any flights heading to LAX?" I asked.

"Sure," said the ticket agent, "there's one leaving in fifteen minutes. I'm pretty sure you can make it."

"Great! How much is the ticket?"

"$250 one way…but if you want to get a round trip ticket it would be cheaper."

"Hell no! I'm never coming back to the ATL."

"Well, I'm sorry you feel that way…" the country girl said, "you could have made a lot of money here at one of our strip joints. My brother's the manager at Magic City. Girl, he would love your ass."

"I'm not a dancer! Stop judging me and just give me my damn ticket!" I demanded. "$250 please!"

As I looked into my purse to search for my wallet, I was stunned to see all of the diamonds blinging in my bag. I damn near dropped my purse, as I stood in shock staring at the diamond Rolex, diamond rings, and diamond studs. Not to mention, two wallets filled with cash.

"Oh my God…" I mumbled. I was horrified.

I knew that Juicy had struck again and this time it was nothing small. It looked like Juicy had robbed a jewelry store.

"Oh God…" I said again, feeling queasy as my forehead began to sweat.

"Something wrong?" asked the ticket agent. "The plane's boarding now."

"No…No…" I said, quickly exchanging cash for the ticket.

I grabbed the ticket and started running toward the plane as fast as I could. Desperate, I pulled out my sunglasses and a hat in an effort to disguise myself—not knowing if I was wanted by the law, the underworld or both.

As I boarded the plane heavy in thought, the Caucasian man wearing a dark business suit tapped me on the shoulder and said, "Excuse me, miss."

Startled, I immediately turned to the man and blurted, "It wasn't me!"

"Excuse me?" asked the man with a confused look on his face, "I was just asking if you could put my briefcase in the overhead."

"Oh...oh...yes," I said greatly relieved.

I tossed his briefcase into the overhead and quickly took my seat. Once the plane was cleared for take-off and the old lady who was sitting beside me wearing thick glasses fell asleep, I slowly began to examine the contents of the bag with a critical eye— realizing that the jewelry was very, very expensive.

"Oh God," I said, dropping my head. "What am I going to do with this jewelry?"

I contemplated giving it back to whomever it belonged to, but I didn't know who it belonged to because I had no idea who Juicy was entertaining. Chance and Trillion knew, but I never wanted to talk to Trillion or Chance again. I even pondered a moment, wondering if either of the girls knew that Juicy stole the jewelry, but I quickly dismissed the thought because Juicy always works alone.

Mia was filled with guilt, sadness and disappointment on the trip back to Los Angeles. Mia couldn't understand why she was dealt this deck of cards. All she ever wanted was to love and be loved. Mia could not understand why her booty, Juicy, had to be exactly what people expected it to be.

A seductress.

A thief.

A slut.

A whore.

Maybe I was Juicy and Juicy was me. Two personalities.

One being—sharing the same cover. But so different from each other.

I thought maybe this world was made for Juicy, and not for me. Juicy seemed to be able to handle it better than me. I wish I could leave and let Juicy live in this cold ass world. They're two of a kind but I quickly refrained from that thinking and just the thought of leaving Juicy with my baby, Janiah, made me puke. All I wanted to do was to make sure that Janiah never turned out to be anything like me, and to make sure that no one ever hurt her. I lived for Janiah—no matter how tormented I had been.

chapter

23

"ELCOME TO LOS ANGELES, CALIFORNIA," said the pilot who came on the intercom announcing our arrival into the City of Angels. Instantly, I woke up and prepared myself to get off the plane. I was relieved to be back in L.A., and finally felt safe. Though I must admit, I also felt a little guilty.

I got away untouched. Or have I?

What goes around comes around, but I hope the circle doesn't end with me. Trillion and Chance are much more responsible for whatever happened this weekend. I plead innocent to whatever damage Juicy caused. Simply put, it wasn't me. And this was my line of reasoning so that I could go on with my life. I needed to go on.

When the plane stopped, I turned on my cell phone and called Janiah.

"Hello," said Janiah.

"Hi Honey. This is Mommy," I said. "I just landed and I'll be coming to get you in about an hour."

"Good!"

"I'm so happy to hear your voice, baby," I said. "I love you so much. I missed you so much!"

"Mommy," she said, "you've only been gone two days. What's wrong with you?"

"I'm fine," I said trying to reassure her. "Did you have fun with Auntie Ducky?"

"Yeah…she's been drilling the hell out of me with all of her sex questions."

"What do you mean?"

"She keeps telling me that I have a booty just like you and she doesn't believe that I'm not having sex."

Damn, I thought, *they're judging my baby just like they judged me.*

"Don't pay them no mind. You know they're all crazy," I reassured her. "Just be ready. I'll be there soon."

When I hung up the phone, I did a quick check of my voicemail. There were several more messages from Trillion, which I deleted before listening to them. Luke had also left me a couple of messages telling me how much he missed me and letting me know that he would be back in town tomorrow.

I felt a bit emotional after listening to Luke's messages. I wanted him so bad—even needed him, but I knew I couldn't tell him anything about Juicy and this past weekend. While I listened to the rest of the voicemails from family, my call waiting kept beeping.

Trillion calling.

Trillion calling.

Trillion calling.

I just let the calls roll into voicemail, as I got off the plane, collected my bags and caught a taxicab back to the house—where I quickly dropped off my things and ran to scoop up Janiah, who was only 10 minutes away from where I lived.

I blew the horn as I waited on Janiah—who didn't come out for several minutes. Instead, NeNe and Ducky came with a whole bunch of questions.

"So…how was the conference?" NeNe asked with a big grin. "I heard that you took that slut, Trillion, with you to the meeting," blurted Ducky.

Just as she spoke Trillion's name, she called again, back to back.

Trillion calling.

Trillion calling.

"I'm tired as hell," I said, "go get Janiah so I can get out of here."

"When are you going to open your eyes and see that fake ass Bitch don't like you?"

I wanted to break down and tell them they were so right! I wanted to confide in them and tell them what happened this weekend, but I didn't remember enough to tell them.

What would I tell them?

I blacked out on Friday and woke up on Sunday carrying a portable jewelry store in my purse. I couldn't reconcile that. I also didn't have a good explanation for my pussy feeling like it was tore up. My jaw was tight, and sore. I could barely swallow. My legs hurt. My back hurt and my rectum was a little bruised. The fear of trying to explain my unusual predicament with Juicy on my backside, would put me at great risk of them committing me to the koo koo house.

"See you guys!" I said rolling up the window on them when I saw Janiah coming out of the house.

"Hey mom!" said Janiah jumping in the front seat, giving me a kiss on the cheek and popping in her new CD.

"Hey baby!" I said.

Within seconds, the music blared through the speakers! Holy mother of God!

It was somebody's new booty song.

"I don't feel like listening to that crazy booty shit!"

Between my sisters telling me about Trillion's tricky ass, Janiah playing that loud music, and my phone blowing up with Trillion's calls, I wanted to scream out loud in that moment. But as soon as I drove into my driveway and stepped out of my car— I smiled.

Roses at my doorstep. "Aaaaaawwwww," I said melting inside.

"Who left you flowers?" Janiah asked, picking up the card. "Probably my friend, Luke."

"You're right," said Janiah, passing the card to me which read—
From your dear friend, Luke.
I miss you baby.

"Mommy," Janiah inquired, "is that your new man? Is that my new daddy?"

"Shut up girl! Get inside that house and get to cleaning." "Okay mom."

"And don't forget to let me know what time we have to be at your new school next week."

"You going to miss me when I leave for school?"

"Hell yeah…" I said laughing, "I'm going to miss you cleaning this house and being my slave."

"Mom…I'm really going to miss you."

"Just get that degree and become the best lawyer L.A. has ever seen!"

"I will, mom!" she said, "and I'll fight for everybody's right and I won't judge anyone! Ever!"

As I looked around the house, I didn't know where to begin. The best place to begin—unloading this heavy purse filled with hot goods. I pulled out all of the jewelry and cash and pulled out Janiah's College Fund Box, which was situated in the back of the closet.

I deposited the stolen goods while offering a silent prayer.

God.

Please forgive me.

I hope you understand.

I ain't no thief.

I sat on the bed and tried to unwind, but I couldn't come down all the way. Though I was exhausted from this weekend, I was still a bit uptight. Just then, my phone began to ring again. I rolled my eyes thinking it was Trillion's stink ass, but to my surprise, it was my baby Luke.

"Hey baby," I said.

"Hello sexy," he crooned in that deep voice. "Thank you for the flowers!"

"No problem. I was sitting in my hotel room thinking about you."

"Are you home yet?" I asked him.

"I'll be back in the morning," he said. "Can I see you tomorrow afternoon? I couldn't stop thinking about you on this trip. I wish I would have brought you."

I wish you would have too, Mia thought to herself, *would have saved me a lot of trouble.*

Trillion was still calling.

Trillion calling.

"Come by tomorrow afternoon." Mia said. "So you won't be at work?"

"No, I'm on vacation," I said.

"Cool sexy. Can't wait to see you again."

When I got off the phone, I couldn't help but to listen to one of Trillion's messages. The message was short, simple and urgent.

Mia.

Call me.

It's very important.

At that moment I started to worry a little, because maybe Trillion did have some information about the jewelry and the cash. Maybe she knew the story behind it, though I didn't feel comfortable enough with her to trust anything she said because the Trillion I know always exaggerates everything. She always lies to every guy she meets, giving him fake names or contact. So, I know there's probably no trail leading back to our real identity from this weekend.

But that was beside the point, I knew in that moment I needed to find a real doctor, a psychiatrist, who could help me. I grabbed the Yellow Pages and started sifting through volumes of names and numbers, writing them down.

I started to get sleepy and before I knew it, I was out.

Next thing I knew, it was morning and Janiah was slamming the door off to school!

I jumped up and knew that I had to clean myself up and this house before Luke came. And I especially wanted to clean the kitchen table—thinking about the last time Luke was here.

Luke was here before I knew it. I greeted him at the door wearing some sexy lingerie. The lingerie was on "purpose." I answered the door with a Kool-Aid smile.

"Hello Mia," he said, "you still in your pajamas, baby?" He kissed me.

I couldn't help but kiss him back. It was a long, wet, juicy kiss.

"Luke," I said. "Come on in and have a seat." "I brought you a souvenir from Vegas."

"Wow!" I said, acknowledging this gold heart chain.

I don't need no more damn jewelry, I thought myself, but instead I offered him a thank you kiss on the cheek.

"Did you have fun in Vegas?" I asked. "Not really," he said. "It was all business."

"So you don't have to say what happens in Vegas stays in Vegas?"

"Mia, if you were there...maybe so. But not this trip," he said with a laugh.

I took Luke by the hand and led him to the kitchen table, where I hoped to rekindle old memories.

"Coffee?" I asked. "No thanks, babe."

"Can I get you anything to drink?"

"No thanks," he said seemingly oblivious to my flirtation. "Can I get you *anything?*" I asked suggestively, bending down to reveal cleavage.

He smiled.

"Just seeing you has made my day..." he said with a big smile. "Now I can go off to work."

"You going to work, *now?*" I asked, disappointed.

"Yes, I have a meeting to be at in thirty minutes, but I would love to take you out for dinner tonight."

"Dinner it is," I said, closing up the lingerie.

chapter

24

I COULDN'T WAIT TO GO OUT with Luke tonight. I spent about an hour in the closet looking for my sexiest outfit.

I found it—a hot, yellow dress that fit every curve on my body with a plunging neckline and sequence on the neckline. I bet he won't ignore me tonight.

My phone started ringing again.

Trillion calling.

Trillion calling.

Damn, I thought to myself. I might have to change my number.

I couldn't let the drama of the day distract me from what I needed to do. I had to find a good psychiatrist and set up an appointment. I started to shuffle through the papers and look over the numbers that I had written down last night. I dialed the first number on the list, when I was suddenly interrupted by the thunderous sound of loud banging on my front door.

It scared the daylights out of me.

I wanted to get my gun—but it was in the dashboard of my car. So instead, I ran straight to the kitchen and grabbed a butcher knife and headed cautiously toward the door.

"Who the hell is it?" I shouted, trying to sound really tough. "Trillion!" she shouted back. "Damn," I said, snatching the door with the knife still in hand.

"Girl…what the hell you doing banging on my door like this!" Trillion caught sight of the knife, and immediately apologized. "Mia, I'm so sorry, but you've been ignoring all of my phone calls. Did you listen to any of the messages I left for you?"

"Just one of your stupid ass messages saying it was urgent that I call you."

"Why didn't you call me back?" she demanded.

"I'm through with you, Trillion!" I said on the edge of anger.

"You can't be through with me because those Niggahs we met in ATL is looking for us."

"What do you mean?" I questioned, "I didn't meet no Niggahs in the ATL."

"You might be right about that," Trillion said, "but Juicy damn sure met them!"

"I'm not even trying to go there with you," I said, "you are so fucked up! You set me up!"

"No Mia…I didn't set you up…it was Chance that invited Juicy to the party."

"How did Chance know anything about Juicy, Trillion?"

"Well…ummmm…. I did tell her that when you drink or take drugs…you kind of change."

"I'm so done with you! Lose my number and forget that you ever knew me!" I shouted.

"I'm so sorry, Mia. I had no idea it would go this far." "What do you mean this far?"

"Those Niggahs are saying we stole their jewelry and money, and they want it back now."

"What jewelry?" I asking, thinking to myself, fuck.

"I didn't take the shit," said Trillion, "and Chance said she didn't take the shit, either."

"I don't got the shit, either."

"But Mia…" protested Trillion, "my shit and Chance's shit also came up missing."

"Well…maybe my shit is missing, too. I haven't even had time to check."

"Maybe Juicy took the shit and you just don't remember," Trillion suggested.

"I ain't got the shit. Juicy ain't got the shit, and you better get the fuck off my steps because I'm done, Trillion. I'm done."

"Mia…those Niggahs in the ATL ain't no joke, baby. I suggest you look for it."

I hated Trillion in this moment. She was someone that I loved and trusted.

"Trillion, get off my step before I call the police and have them escort you out of here."

"Fuck you, Mia! I ain't going down for you!"

I slammed the door in Trillion's face, and watched as she slowly backed away from my step. In that moment, I really wanted to give Trillion the jewelry back, but since I could not trust ANYTHING that came out of her mouth, I could not confide in her. For all I knew, maybe her and Chance wanted the jewelry for themselves. For a quick second, I wondered if she would "give me up" and rat me out to the guys, but I reasoned to myself that deep down inside, Trillion knew that this was all her fault.

I was so pissed that Trillion had come to my door still lying and bringing all of this bullshit to my house. Though I must admit, I was a little nervous and hoped that all of this would blow over. I could barely think about anything else, and didn't even hear the door when Janiah came home from school.

I was standing in the kitchen, when I turned around and saw her—scared the daylights out of me.

"Mom," said Janiah holding her hand against her head, "do you have anything for my head? I have a bad headache."

Damn, I thought to myself. *I sure don't want her to get sick now, especially since I got this hot date tonight.*

"Sure baby," I said reaching for some Benadryl. "It must be your sinuses…take two of these and they will make you sleep."

"Thanks mom."

"I have a date tonight," I said, "but if you're not feeling good…I can cancel and stay home with you tonight."

"No," she said, "I will be fine, mom. You need to find you a good man, especially since I'm leaving for college this year."

"Okay love, just rest."

"Sure I will, after I watch my favorite television show."

🌺

With the drama of the day, the afternoon passed quickly. Before I knew it—it was time to shower and get dressed. I showered and sprayed on my finest cologne. I checked my watch and knew that Luke would be pulling up soon. No sooner than I had thought, the phone rang and it was Luke telling me he was right around the corner and that I could come outside.

I went into the bedroom where Janiah lay resting. "How you feeling, baby?"

"I'm better…"

"Okay I'm leaving…come lock the door," I told her. "Mommy…you have the key, so lock the door. I'm watching my favorite show."

"Get your butt up and come lock the deadbolt."

I locked the bottom and could only hope that girl gets up and locks this deadbolt.

With that, I jumped into Luke's Mercedes and we were off. I leaned over and kissed him, offering a warm greeting and a big Kool Aid smile. "Hello honey."

"Baby, do you like seafood?" he asked. "Sure…it's my favorite kind of food."

"Well, I'm treating you to the best seafood in town." "Where we going?"

"Santa Monica…right on the water." "Oh cool!" I shouted with enthusiasm.

Luke held my hand all the way to the restaurant. As we arrived, the valet immediately opened the door, helping me to exit. I could feel Luke's eyes on me the second I stood up.

"Baby…you are so damn fine in that yellow dress!" he said, "and you smell good, too!"

"Thank you, Lukie!" I said, grinning all of the way into the restaurant.

We were seated quickly at the best table in the restaurant. From our table, we had the most perfect ocean view. The restaurant was dimmed with candles and was absolutely beautiful. Champagne was set up on the table along with a seafood platter filled with lobster, crabs, oysters and steak. Wow! I knew that Luke had gone the extra mile and set this whole scene up. And to my surprise, even the waitress greeted Luke and I, both by name.

"Hi Luke and Mia," she said, "My name is Sally."

I looked at Luke and smiled—obviously he was a regular. "Champagne?" he offered.

"I don't drink," I said, "so you can have it all."

"I don't drink, either," he said, throwing up his hand. "Luke…you are the best," I said, "you didn't have to go through all of this trouble for me."

"Mia, I did…because you mean so much to me. I can't get you off my mind."

"I can't stop thinking about you, either."

"Mia, you are the woman I have been looking for all of these years" he said, "I always dreamed about a beautiful woman…with a beautiful body and intelligent mind."

"Thank you…"

"I call that the BBB," he said with a wide grin. "What do you mean the BBB?"

"Baby…it's something that's very rare. Brains. Beauty and a Big'ole Booty."

I laughed out loud.

"I didn't think you cared for my booty."

"Well Mia," he said, "ain't nothing wrong with having a little dessert to go along with the main course."

Mia blushed.

"I want you to know that I'm very proud of a woman who has a body like yours but didn't fall into the trap of using it to get what she wants. You are a rare breed."

"Thank you, baby," I said to him, while thinking to myself, *he wouldn't be saying that if he met Juicy.*

"That's why I want to snatch you up…" he said, "and ask you if you're interested in being in a committed relationship with me. You can confide in me about anything."

I would have loved to take him up on his offer, but I knew that first, I would need help.

"I really love the man that you are. You are the kind of man that I've always imagined myself settling down with, but I do want to take my time and get to know you and you really get to know me."

"No rush baby…I'm not going anywhere and you can't either. Don't forget…you're stuck with me for at least another year…you signed a lease, remember?"

I laughed.

We were both starving and began to enjoy the feast that was on our table. Luke started feeding me, and I reciprocated his affection by feeding him back. The heat between us began to rise. We couldn't wait to touch each other again. All I wanted to do was to make love to Luke in a very special way.

We talked. Ate.

Laughed.

And felt each other up till the stroke of midnight.

It was as though nothing else existed except for he and I—and all that we wanted was each other.

"Are you ready to go back to my place?" I offered.

"Sure baby…I've been waiting for that suggestion all night."

Sally had dropped off the check about an hour before and was staring at us from a distance. You could tell she was so ready for us to leave. By the time we got outside, the Valet was closed and Luke's car was sitting right in front of the restaurant with the keys in it.

Everybody had gone home except me, Luke and Sally. Luke left an extra-large tip for Sally's patience.

As we drove back to my place, all I could think about was making love to Luke, but I would have to do it "quietly" 'cause I certainly couldn't wake up Janiah.

I also thought about letting my guard down and telling Luke everything.

No more secrets.

Maybe Luke was God sent.

I even contemplated calling Trillion's stink-ass, and giving the jewelry back and washing my hands clean of all the drama. I daydreamed of starting my life over. Who knows? Maybe one day I might even marry Luke.

As Luke's car turned onto the street, we immediately noticed there were several police cars with flashing lights, and an ambulance parked right in front of Luke's building.

"What the fuck!" said Luke. There were so many policemen.

"Luke, what kind of people do you have living in this building?"

"Baby, I don't know what's going on."

Luke didn't even park—he turned onto the sidewalk and jumped out of the car. I quickly followed as we headed toward my front door, and I was shocked to find that my unit was the focus of all the attention.

Janiah, I screamed!

There were two officers posted right outside my door, and as Luke and I approached, Luke began to converse with the officers… but I ran right through them. A female officer who was posted just outside the door reached for my arm, but I slipped straight through her grasp, almost knocking her over.

"Ma'am…we're securing the premises. You have to stay back!" "I live here!" I screamed, "where's my daughter?" bogarting my way inside.

The apartment was demolished. Turned upside down.

The whole place had been ransacked. The couch was flipped over. Lamps broken.

Kitchen table destroyed.

I panicked as I ran toward Janiah's bedroom where I saw two paramedics leaning over her lifeless body, as she lay in a pool of blood.

Janiah!

Janiah!

Four cops had to hold me back, while Luke burst through the officers and grabbed me to take me out of the house. He grabbed me, holding me tight and we both cried.

"Baby, let them take her to the hospital," he cried out. "Is she dead?" I screamed.

"She's going to be okay," said Luke, "but they need to get her to the hospital. Give me your phone and let me call your mother."

What happened?

What happened?

What happened?

"The officer said it was a robbery," said Luke, "and they also think your daughter might have been raped."

I collapsed.

chapter

25

THE NEXT THING I REMEMBER is standing in the middle of the lobby at the hospital. Luke and I were in the waiting room. Janiah was admitted into the hospital and the doctors were examining her. I was so close to the edge that I knew at any minute, I was about to fall off—especially when the doctor came out to talk to Luke and I.

"Are you Janiah's mother?" asked the tall, Caucasian man wearing the long white coat.

"Yes," I said desperately, standing to meet him. "How is she?" "She's been beaten pretty bad...and she's been raped."

I went into shock and convulsions. "Oh my God!" buckling at the knees.

Luke grabbed me and was holding me up, trying to support me. In this moment, the room went black and all I could think about was getting revenge on the bastards who had done this—all of them.

I could hear Janiah from the other room, and the doctor escorted me in to see her. Her eyes were black and blue and her lips were swollen. She was going in and out of consciousness. As I stood over her bed, a female detective entered the room and asked if she could interview Janiah. I could barely respond myself as Janiah began to wake up.

"Could you please get out of the room! My baby just got raped!"

"Mia," said Luke, "let them help us."

"The sooner we get some information. The sooner we catch these monsters," said the cop.

"She's unconscious!" I protested.

"Well, can we interview you?" she asked. Reluctantly, I nodded.

"Do you have enemies?" she asked. "No," I said. "Why do you ask that?"

"Because…this crime scene looks like a deliberate set-up. Revenge of some kind."

"Revenge on a kid…" Luke cried out, "come on, man!"

Tears began to drop from my eyes because I did not have any ideas but Juicy sure did.

"Let's continue this later," suggested Luke, "her family will be here soon and maybe they can help with some information."

Janiah began to wake up and sat up, panicked in the bed. "Mommy! Mommy! They hurt me!"

Mia held Janiah tight.

"Mommy's here," I promised, "No one will ever hurt you again."

"There were three of them," said Janiah, crying hysterically. "They said they were looking for Juicy."

The cop intervened.

"Who's Juicy?" the cop asked me directly.

"You know people like this, Mia?" Luke asked in outrage and disbelief.

"No!" I screamed.

"Who in the hell is Juicy?" cried Luke.

"Does Juicy have a last name?" asked the cop.

"Is Juicy one of your home girls?" Luke chimed in. "Where we can find Juicy?" the officer asked.

No!

No!

No!

"Who in the fuck is Juicy?" Ida Mae asked, entering the room with the rest of my family.

The family was devastated. My father, sisters and brothers all gathered around Janiah's bed with tears streaming their cheeks.

"What did you let happen to my grandchild?" Ida Mae shouted.

"Mama…they raped Janiah."

"Baby…what Niggahs did you owe money to?" my mother asked.

My daddy couldn't take it anymore. He looked at me and promised, "Don't worry baby…I'll find them and settle this."

When my father left, Ida Mae reached out and grabbed me holding me tight. This was the first time that I had ever been comforted by my mother. In this moment, I completely surrendered to my mother's love and embrace. I broke down, resembling little more than a child myself. I was three years old again, and now my mother was here to help me to deal with this.

"Get her out of here, Luke," said Ida Mae, "I'll take care of Janiah," she promised.

Shaking, Luke escorted me out of the room, but we didn't get too far before we were stopped by the police.

"Ma'am…we need more information about Juicy," the officer said.

I couldn't take anymore.

"I don't know Juicy!" was all I could say, running out of the hospital feeling the burden of my conscious. The guilt had all but consumed me.

"Stop, Mia!" Luke asked, chasing behind me. "I have to go home!"

"For what?"

I didn't respond.

"Just take me home!" I commanded.

As I got in the car, Luke began to question me more than the officers.

"Do you have any enemies, baby?" he asked.

I looked up at Luke with tears streaming down my cheeks. "I won't have any after tonight."

Luke's face lit up with surprise.

The rest of the ride home was silent. When we pulled up, I jumped out of his car and ran to mine. Luke was close on my heels, as he watched me open my glove box and pull out my gun.

"Mia! I got this!" he said, "You can't do this!" He tried to grab me, but I resisted.

"No! Move out of my way, Luke. They all have to die." "Please Mia, let me take care of this. I'll call my boys." "No!" I insisted.

"I won't let you do this!" said Luke, grabbing hold of the gun. "Someone has to die! Someone has to die!" I screamed, fighting him off. We began to wrestle, and I knew this was escalating into a dangerous situation. Luke also knew, so in a flash, he twisted my arm and immediately I released it to him. "I'll take care of it. Trust me…" he said.

I surrendered and ran inside, into my bathroom, and locked the door.

In that moment, I did not want to live anymore. Why was God allowing this to happen to me?

Why?

Why?

I knew in this moment, I would be better off dead than alive. I couldn't allow Juicy to do any more damage, not only to myself, but to those who I loved the most. I had several prescription sleeping pills in my cabinet and I took every pill in the cabinet. Within moments, I began to get queasy and my head started to pound. I dropped to my knees and began to call out.

God!

God!

God!

I could feel a war waging within—Juicy was coming back. The pills had called her back. "I hate you! I hate you! Why did you do this?" Mia screamed at Juicy. "Back at you, Bitch!" squealed Juicy. "I hate you, too!" "I will get rid of you this time!"

"I told your stupid ass you should have let me run your life! But no…you wanted to prove to the world that you were better than me!"

"Shut up! Shut up!" screamed Mia, hysterically.

"People in this world will always judge you!" promised Juicy, "you can't win this war, Bitch!"

"I will win this one!" I screamed, reaching for the razorblade on the sink.

"Hell naw!" screamed Juicy, as Mia began to slit her wrists. Juicy and Mia began to wrestle with the blade.

Mia pulled the blade to her skin.
Juicy pushed it away.
Mia pulled.
Juicy pushed.
Pulled.
Pushed.

"Help me, God! Please God let me die!" Mia screamed.
Help me, God!
Help me, God!
God!

And with that, the bathroom got brighter and brighter. Peace filled the room as the deep voice of God echoed throughout the walls.

MY CHILD.
I WILL HELP YOU.

BUT YOU MUST PROMISE SOMETHING…AND I PROMISE THAT I WILL REMOVE THIS DEMON FROM YOU.

Mia trembled in awe of the voice.

"What do you want me to promise?" she asked.

THAT YOU WILL GIVE YOUR LIFE TO ME AND BECOME MY SOLDIER, A MINISTER.

"I will do whatever you ask!" I said desperately.

The light got brighter and brighter until Mia began to violently throw up green vomit splattering all over the walls, shaking, convulsing and breaking out in a cold sweat. The essence of Juicy stood up, and walked out of Mia's body into the atmosphere.

Mia collapsed onto the floor. Exhausted.

But free. Meanwhile…

Ten minutes later, Janiah suffered another anxiety attack as doctors and nurses tried to calm her. They quickly ushered Ida Mae and all family members from the room. Janiah began to convulse and shake with tremors. They could not seem to calm her body, which broke into a violent sweat.

"Let's get some Demerol going!" shouted the doctor.

The nurse quickly inserted a bag of Demerol into Janiah's IV, turning it on full throttle. Within moments, Janiah grabbed her head. "My head hurts!" she screamed, as the medication was pumped into her veins. As her young body began to relax, Janiah began to smile at everyone in the room.

The nurses and doctors were intrigued by the transition in her personality, as she began to wink to the men in the room. As Janiah lay back and closed her eyes—she began to hear an unusual voice that seemed to come from somewhere deep inside of hers.

Hey girl!

My name is JUICY!

I'm your BOOTY and I got your back!

I need you to listen to me…I can make you rich and powerful and get you everything you think you want in life…but ONLY if you allow me to be me!

I'm your best friend, Janiah!

I see the whole wide world looking at you, Janiah!

You have the front view of life and I have the rear view! I will call guys over to you, Janiah.

I will rub up against the ones that need to be rubbed. I'll suck the ones that need to be sucked.

I'll fuck the ones that need to be fucked.

Because a booty's gotta do what a booty's gotta do.

Juicy laughed. And laughed. And laughed.

Juicy's never die. We only multiply.

Always remember...
in "using what you got to get what you want,"
there are consequences that live beyond the moment.
Everything that you do eventually returns to you...
and sometimes, to the ones you love.

Don't Judge A Booty By Its Cover

Made in the USA
Middletown, DE
23 December 2021

56767125R00119